THE CASE
OF THE
CRYPTIC CRINOLINE

THE CASE
OF THE
CRYPTIC CRINOLINE

AN ENOLA HOLMES MYSTERY

NANCY SPRINGER

PHILOMEL BOOKS

PENGUIN YOUNG READERS GROUP

PHILOMEL BOOKS
A division of Penguin Young Readers Group.
Published by The Penguin Group.
Penguin Group (USA) Inc., 375 Hudson Street, New York, NY 10014, U.S.A.
Penguin Group (Canada), 90 Eglinton Avenue East, Suite 700, Toronto, Ontario M4P 2Y3,
Canada (a division of Pearson Penguin Canada Inc.).
Penguin Books Ltd, 80 Strand, London WC2R 0RL, England.
Penguin Ireland, 25 St. Stephen's Green, Dublin 2, Ireland (a division of Penguin Books Ltd).
Penguin Group (Australia), 250 Camberwell Road, Camberwell, Victoria 3124, Australia
(a division of Pearson Australia Group Pty Ltd).
Penguin Books India Pvt Ltd, 11 Community Centre, Panchsheel Park, New Delhi—110 017, India.
Penguin Group (NZ), 67 Apollo Drive, Rosedale, North Shore 0632, New Zealand
(a division of Pearson New Zealand Ltd).
Penguin Books (South Africa) (Pty) Ltd, 24 Sturdee Avenue,
Rosebank, Johannesburg 2196, South Africa.
Penguin Books Ltd, Registered Offices: 80 Strand, London WC2R 0RL, England.

Published simultaneously in Canada. Printed in the United States of America.
Design by Marikka Tamura. Text set in Cochin.

Library of Congress Cataloging-in-Publication Data
Springer, Nancy. The case of the cryptic crinoline : an Enola Holmes mystery / Nancy Springer.
p. cm. Summary: In late-nineteenth-century London, fourteen-year-old Enola Holmes,
much younger sister of detective Sherlock Holmes, turns to Florence Nightingale for help when
her investigation into the disappearance of a Crimean War widow grows cold.
[1. Mystery and detective stories. 2. Missing persons—Fiction. 3. Characters in literature—
Fiction. 4. Nightingale, Florence, 1820–1910—Fiction. 5. London (England)—History—
1800–1950—Fiction. 6. Great Britain—History—Victoria, 1837–1901—Fiction.] I. Title.
PZ7.S76846Care 2009 [Fic]—dc22 2008040475
ISBN 978-0-399-24781-1
1 3 5 7 9 10 8 6 4 2

To my mother

Scutari, Turkey, 1855

(The faint of heart may proceed directly to Chapter the First.)

ON THE HILLTOP ABOVE THE HARBOUR STANDS THE huge square building that used to be the barracks for the Turkish army, but is now Hell's home on earth. The stench of bloated carcasses—cow, horse, human—floating in the sea is nothing compared with the stench within that massive masonry cube. Shoulder to shoulder on its stone floors lie wounded, sick, or dying men, mostly young British soldiers, many without even a straw pallet beneath them or a blanket for covering. Hell is relatively quiet; so deeply desperate, helpless, and weak are the patients that they languish almost soundless, dying by the thousands of infection, gangrene, and cholera.

One of those lying insensible, not likely to live through the approaching night, is a young fellow just twenty years of age. By his side crouches a frightened girl even younger than he, his bride of less than a year, who has come to this awful place with him. Most of the men's wives have come along, trailing the regiments with babes in arms, for no way is provided for the soldiers to send home their pay, and separated from their husbands the women will starve.

Many of them are starving anyway.

Watching her husband die, the girl maintains the mute, shivering, and mostly silent misery character- istic of Scutari, for she has seen too much death; she realises that she herself might well die, and she does not dare to hope that the new life she carries within her thin body can survive.

A little farther down the ward, a woman wearing a shapeless grey wrapper and cap washes crusted mucus from a soldier's eyes. Since recently arriving from England, the small group of determined nurses has managed somewhat to improve matters in Scu- tari. They have scrubbed filthy floors, bathed filthy bodies, boiled the lice out of some of the blankets. The soldier with the infected eyes may go blind, but, as fewer than half of those who enter Scutari come out alive, he should consider himself lucky.

"Keep your hands away from your eyes, now," the nurse tells him, "no matter how much you wish to rub them, for your touch transfers foul matter into them."

Walking through the eight miles of wards comes another nurse, a thin, aristocratic woman who carries a lamp, for night is falling. Her oval face is remarkably sweet, symmetrical, and placid. Her hair, parted precisely in the middle, lies smooth like brown wings beneath a white lace cap that ties under her chin. Slowly she progresses, pausing at the foot of many a patient's pallet and speaking in a soft, melodious voice. "The letter to your mother has been sent, Higgins. . . . Not at all, you are very welcome. Did you eat today, O'Reilly? Good. I should have a blanket for you tomorrow. Did you use a fresh sponge, Walters?" As she pauses where the nurse ministers to the man going blind: "Good. Go to your quarters, now; it's getting dark."

As the nurse leaves, the Lady with the Lamp walks forward again, to pause where the trembling girl crouches beside her unconscious husband. After a look at him, the lady sets down her lamp, seats herself likewise on the cold stone floor, takes the man's blue bare feet into her lap, and begins briskly to rub them with her hands, perhaps warming them a bit.

"It is the only comfort I can give him," she tells the girl, who sits mute and huge-eyed by his side. "You must go now, child. You may come back in the morning."

The thin young wife gazes back at her, wordless and imploring.

3

The lady replies to that gaze as if to a spoken plea. "I know you wish to stay with him, child, but the rule is that there are to be no females in the wards at night, and if we do not obey, the army may send us back to the kitchen or, even worse, back to England." Her soft voice never rises, and her face, although thin, shows no weariness, resentment, or frustration; it remains angelically serene even as she says, "If that happens, then there will be no nursing for the unfortunates, not even in the daytime. So we must go. Do you understand?"

And, assuming that the girl can hear her, perhaps she thinks the child does understand. Although the younger woman fails to move, there is no defiance in her eyes, only wretched exhaustion.

"Come." Placing the dying man's feet gently back on the floor, the lady takes her lamp and rises. "Come, I will walk with you and light your way." She offers the girl her hand, and after a moment the young bride reaches up to accept that warm grip. The older woman helps her to her feet. For a moment the two of them stand, hand in hand, over the—one might as well call it a body.

The girl's thin lips move three times before, with an odd plangent abruptness, she speaks. "'E's my 'usband," she states helplessly and unnecessarily.

"I know, dear, but you still cannot—"

"'E's a good man," the girl goes on without seeming to hear. "'Is name is Tupper. Thomas Tupper. Somebody besides me oughter remember."

"Yes, of course they should," soothes the Lady with the Lamp. Those who survive Scutari will make famous the comfort of her quiet voice. "Come along now, Mrs. Thomas Tupper."

CHAPTER
THE
FIRST

"Miss Meshle," said Mrs. Tupper as she took my empty plate away, "if ye 'ave time to set an' talk a while . . ."

Before my elderly, deaf-as-a-dumpling landlady finished the sentence, she had my fullest attention, because she spoke softly instead of shouting as she usually did, but mostly because, due to her deafness, any attempt at conversation was most unusual. Indeed, her request to "talk" was unprecedented. Generally, after one of her frugal suppers (tonight, spring onions being in season, it had been fish-and-onion soup with bread pudding), I would give her a nod of thanks and retreat behind the closed door of my room, where I could rid myself of the poufs, baubles, and underpinnings of "Miss Meshle," sit in my overstuffed armchair with my feet upon a hassock, and be comfortable.

"I could use a bit of advice," Mrs. Tupper continued as she took the white crockery soup tureen and placed it on the stove as if it were a pot, then scraped leftover bread pudding into the slop pail rather than into the cat's dish. Greatly wondering what ailed her, I nodded and gestured, signalling my willingness to listen.

"Let's go set down," Mrs. Tupper said.

I was, of course, already sitting, at the table, but we moved to the shabby "parlour suite" at the other end of Mrs. Tupper's single room—her house, although clean, was little more than a hovel—and there, as I took a chair, Mrs. Tupper hunched on the edge of the horsehair sofa, fixing me with her watery grey gaze.

"It hain't none of my business, but I've noticed there's more to you than meets the eye," she said as if she felt it necessary to explain why she would confide in such a youngster. "You hain't just a working-girl like you seems to be, not when ye can pass as a street beggar or yit a lady to the manor born, an' when ye took sich pains goin' out as a nun—"

I made no attempt to hide my shock; she was not supposed to know this. If word were to reach my brothers, Mycroft and Sherlock, enabling them to locate my place of lodging in London's East End, my freedom would be greatly endangered.

But Mrs. Tupper seemed not to notice my consternation. "—in the dark of night tryin' to 'elp them as is cold an' 'ungry," she went on, "an' where ye get the means, dear only knows." Peering up at me, for she had never been tall, and a dowager's hump had shortened her yet more, she added, "Ye're a good person, Miss Meshle, or whatever yer real name may be—"

"Enola Holmes," I whispered involuntarily. Luckily, she could not possibly hear me and went on without noticing.

"—an' ye're a force t'be reckoned with, an' I'm 'oping ye can 'elp me."

Often enough she had helped *me*, nursing me through colds or fevers or, once, injuries, when a garroter had attacked me. She kept a motherly eye—while I could only imagine what it might be like to have a normal mother, Mrs. Tupper, pressing blood sausage upon me at breakfast and exhorting me out of my fits of melancholia, surely resembled a proper mum. Of course I wanted to help her. "Good heavens," I exclaimed, leaning forward in my turn, "what is wrong?"

Reaching into her apron pocket, she produced an envelope that had evidently come in the day's post, which she handed to me. Nodding and gesturing as if I, not she, were deaf, she encouraged me to open this and read the enclosure.

The daylight from Mrs. Tupper's downstairs window—of which she was rightfully proud, as windows were taxed—the light was waning, but so heavily was the missive printed, in densely black India ink, that I could see it clearly. Slashed across thick paper in the most brutal handwriting I had ever seen, angular and bristling and penned with weapon force, each stroke a club at one end and a rapier at the other, it read:

CARRIER PIGEON. DELIVER YOUR BIRD-BRAINED MESSAGE AT ONCE OR YOU WILL BE SORRY YOU EVER LEFT SCUTARI.

Scutari? Reading the missive twice, I could make no sense of it other than the threat. Yet, as arresting as the message was, the spiked handwriting alarmed me more.

"Do you recognise the writing?" I demanded.

"Eh?" Mrs. Tupper put her ear-trumpet to her ear.

Into it I shouted, "Do you know this hand?" already guessing the answer, for if the anonymous threatener had thought she would know his writing, he would have disguised it, perhaps pasting together letters cut out of newspapers, as was the wont of popular-fiction villains.

"Eh? Know the man? How would I?"

Confound everything, at times such as this I quite wished I could just scribble her a note. But, like most common folk, Mrs. Tupper could read only slowly and with difficulty.

"The *writing*!" I tried again.

"Never seen it. I'd remember, wouldn't I, a thorn-patch like that?" Gesticulating, she expressed alarm and bewilderment. "I think 'e's mistaken me for someone else."

"Maybe," I said doubtfully, as Tupper was hardly a common name. Indeed, I had never met any other Tupper. But it was, of course, her long-dead husband's name, and there might be a few of his surviving relatives in London. "Did Mr. Tupper have family?"

"Eh?" She put the trumpet to her ear.

Into it I bawled, "Mr. Tupper!"

"Died in Scutari." Mrs. Tupper clutched herself as if cold, although it was a fine May evening. "Almost thirty-five years ago an' I'll never forget it. 'Orrible place. Like 'ell on earth."

I lapsed back in my comfortless chair, scolding myself: Scutari. Of course. The British headquarters in Turkey during the Crimean War.

I asked, "Was Mr. Tupper in the army?"

"Eh?"

To spare the gentle reader any more of this, let

me set forth in a straightforward fashion the tale that she told me over the next few hours in a far more confused way, and understandably so, for the Crimean War was one of the most confused conflicts ever undertaken by human stupidity: England and Napoleonic France, of all the unlikely allies, joining with heathen Turkey, even more unlikely, against the already-dying giant that had been Ottoman Russia. "Theirs not to wonder why, theirs but to do or die," doomed men charging straight into cannon-fire for the sake of a godforsaken peninsula in the Black Sea: the Crimea, chiefly occupied by lice the size of spiders, great fat leaping fleas, and rats so big that terriers ran away from them.

Mr. Tupper, however (Mrs. Tupper explained to me), had voyaged to the Crimea as a business venture, being a sumpter, one who sold to soldiers the goods their own thieving suppliers failed to provide for them. Seizing the opportunity, off he went, taking his bride along without a second thought. They were both the merest youngsters. They saw the officers' wives accompanying their husbands with carriage-loads of servants, silverware, and linens, as if going to war were a holiday. Indeed, women by the thousands accompanied the armies, females ranging from camp-followers to Sisters of Mercy, little knowing that most of them, like the men, would die.

Not from battle, but from disease.

"Crimean fever, it were," explained Mrs. Tupper. "There Thomas lay not knowing nothing, with blood running out of 'is ears, 'is eyes, 'is mouth an' nose. Me, trying to 'elp, I paid a couple of the native beggars to lay 'im in an ox-cart for me, an' that way I took 'im to the big 'ospital there at Scutari, ye know." She shook her head, remembering her own innocence. "I thought maybe the doctors an' nurses there could fix 'im up. The word were that they 'ad nurses new from England."

But those nurses, as I was later to learn, were subject to the commands of the army surgeons, who regarded them not only as interfering females in a male domain but, even worse, as civilian spies sent to ruin an otherwise good time with their hen-witted ideas about *caring* for common soldiers. The army placed many restrictions on these annoying women. In the name of propriety, for instance, females were not allowed in the wards at night.

Each morning, then, they needed to remove those who had died since the day before.

Including Mr. Tupper.

"I tidied 'im a bit, sewed 'im up in 'is blanket, an' they put 'im in the same big grave as thirty others done passed away during the dark hours," Mrs. Tupper told me, going on to explain that meanwhile, her livelihood—her husband's goods, tent, pack-ponies, et cetera—had vanished as if into smoke, looted by wartime thieves. Left with no means to get home to England, she found herself amongst others consigned to the very lowest regions of the inferno that was Scutari. Beneath the barracks, or hospital, ran a maze of cellars, and it was here that Mrs. Tupper took refuge along with other widows, orphaned children, crippled old peasants left behind by their families, all manner of beggars—of which she was now one.

"'An me not in the best of 'ealth, either."

But rather than elaborate on this interesting statement, Mrs. Tupper got up to light a few candles. While she was on her feet (no small undertaking, at her age—heavens, she had to be more than fifty!), she opened a carved wooden box I had often noticed, centred as it was upon her sideboard. From this box she brought me a fading photograph to look at. "That were taken of Mr. Tupper an' me on our wedding day," she declared as I studied the posed portrait of two young people in the absurd clothing of mid-century—his vast drooping bow-tie, and her skirt spread wide over hoops and crinolines, like an inverted bowl. My good landlady had lapsed into a reminiscent mood, seeming almost to have forgotten about the frightening letter that had caused her to confide in me in the first place.

Directing her attention back to the black-inked,

brutal missive, I shouted into her ear-trumpet, "What are you supposed to deliver? What message? To whom?"

"I dunno!" Seating herself again, she hugged herself with her skinny arms. "I've thought an' thought an' I just dunno! What with losing the baby an' all, I might've forgot."

An odd, almost seasick, upside-down feeling took hold of me and rendered me speechless. I simply could not imagine . . . my dear old landlady, she who now spent her days stewing oxtails and tatting pillow-slips, had once traveled to a barbaric land, lost her husband, and then, "not in the best of 'ealth" . . .

Mrs. Tupper must have seen myriad shocked questions in my face.

"Stillborn it were," she explained, "an' no wonder, fer I were more'n half starved, my clothes in rags an' no bed to lie on in them caves, an' no sleep to be 'ad, either, for the rats would nibble yer fingers." With her arms still clasped around herself, she rocked her hunched upper body to and fro. "A 'ellish place it was. Folk went mad. One of 'em took my baby an' flung it into the sea. I thought fer sure I would perish, too, an' that grieved I were, I didn't greatly care."

I whispered, "How ever did you escape?"

And there was no need for me to shout in her ear-trumpet, for she understood my question well enough, from my face if not from my lips.

"The English nurse lady it were," she said. "Funny, I hain't thought of 'er in years. Yet she were famous at the time; the soldiers, they called her the Lady with the Lamp. 'Undreds of them she nursed every day like a mother. 'Ow or why she found time to take mercy on me is a miracle." Mrs. Tupper's watery gaze seemed to see not me, but a distant place of the past. "Maybe she 'eard I wouldn't . . ." My landlady's papery old face actually flushed pink. "I wouldn't, if you know what I mean, like them camp-followers. . . . Most of the women in the cellars would do anything for the sake of food an' pennies, an' I don't blame 'em, but I just couldn't bring meself . . . Maybe that were it. 'Owever it come about, one day one of them crippled boys she adopted fetched me to 'er. Up in a corner tower she were, an' me with barely strength to climb the stairs. There must've been a 'undred people in that room, jabbering all French an' whatnot, coming an' going with sponge baths an' bandage lint an' shirt buttons an' lemons an' tincture of iodine an' knitted Cardigans an' Balaclavas an' who knows what all; she 'ad 'er own storehouse in there."

"What was her name?" I murmured, trying to remember—for I, also, had heard of this remarkable Englishwoman, although I must admit that my knowledge of the Crimean War was sorely lacking; my education, dependent upon my father's library, had focussed on Socrates, Plato, Aristotle, and the like.

"She saw to it that I were washed an' fed," marveled Mrs. Tupper, "an' fine clothes she give me, better'n what I was married in, an' she arranged my passage 'ome an' paid for it out of 'er own purse. An' that gracious she were, chatting to me—though I barely understood a word she said. Deaf I was even back then, but I never said nothin', for I 'oped it would go away, bein' just from the gunfire there at Sevastopol, ye see, when Mr. Tupper an' me were taking brandy to the troops while the Russian ladies set up on top of the 'ill with their parasols an' their picnic baskets, watching like it were a music 'all show."

Good heavens. She had been in *battle*, too? My little old landlady?

Hardly knowing what to think or how to continue this rambling interview, I once more lifted the mysterious missive that had come in her post and showed it to her. "Mrs. Tupper," I implored, "do you have any idea—"

She shook her toothless head vehemently. "I just don't know!" she cried. "It don't make no sense. I were nobody over there!"

A very brave nobody, I thought. But still, a mere

accidental woman caught in the war. So who on earth was her mysterious enemy, and what did he — for unmistakably the ferocious handwriting was that of a man — what did he want of her? Now, thirty-four years afterward?

Although my curiosity might never be satisfied, still, I felt it my duty to help her with this mysterious matter.

CHAPTER THE SECOND

So, as every virtuous young lady should do, I sought the advice of an older, wiser, masculine head, consulting a man of the world: Dr. Leslie Ragostin, Scientific Perditorian—my employer.

I jest. Dr. Ragostin was fictitious, my invention so that I should have the opportunity to search for missing things and persons. All the next day, at work as Miss Meshle, the great man's secretary, I puzzled over Mrs. Tupper's problem: how to deal with the sender of her mysteriously threatening letter?

As was my custom, I first sat at my desk and composed a list of questions:

Why "carrier pigeon"? Because she was going home? Are a carrier pigeon and a homing pigeon the same? To call a person a pigeon is a very odd term of insult.

The Americans say "stool pigeon" of an informer. Is, call him X, an American?

"Bird-brained" rather than "hare-brained" also an Americanism?

What message?

From whom?

To whom?

How does it concern X? Does he wish to receive it, intercept it, destroy it?

How has he fixed on Mrs. Tupper?

Was he in Scutari with her?

Unhelpful, overall. I did not really feel that the threatening letter had come from an American. In no way was America concerned in the Crimea; moreover, there was something quite European about X's hedgehog handwriting, including the ink —

I added to the list,

19

Why India ink? Meant for pen-and-ink sketches; is X an artist?

Then I sat scowling at the list without another worthwhile thought until Joddy, the page-boy, came in with the morning's newspapers and, since it was May, a bouquet of lilacs I had requested for the sake of their heavenly scent.

Nor did I achieve anything more that day than to compose, and bang out upon the very modern typewriting machine I had recently purchased, the following to be placed in the newspaper personal advertisements:

```
Carrier pigeon has no message, knows of
no message, can deliver nothing. Further
inquiries pointless. Please desist. Mrs. T.
```

"T" for Tupper; I did not know Mrs. Tupper's first name.

Relieved to find her in the kitchen that evening cooking one of her ghastly messes and none the worse for wear, I showed her this, receiving her permission to place it in the newspapers.

The next day I typed numerous copies, took them around to all the dailies on Fleet Street, and hoped that would be the end of the matter.

Would that it were so.

That was a Wednesday. *Carrier pigeon has no message* was published in the Thursday morning editions. On Thursday evening, as I wended my way back to Mrs. Tupper's ramshackle house crammed between the tenements of the East End, my thoughts were mainly of supper, hoping it would be something at least remotely palatable. I walked up the front steps expecting some aroma—whether of stewed herring, chicken livers, or some less disgusting variety of meat—but the moment I opened the door, all such thoughts fled my mind.

I saw drawers hanging open, chairs overturned, shelves knocked down, crockery broken upon the plank floor.

I smelled cigar smoke, and whale oil leaking from a smashed lamp, and the distressingly physical odour of fear.

I heard the smothered sound of someone crying. "'Elp!" came a muffled feminine voice, sobbing. "Please 'elp me!" The sound scorched my heart, for what despicable sort of villain would distress or harm such a deaf old dear as Mrs. Tupper?

And what else might he do?

Could he be still on the premises?

Snatching my dagger from my bodice—with its hilt disguised as a large, hideous brooch, it nestled between my buttons, sheathed in my corset—with weapon in hand, I entered the ransacked house, looking sharply about me as I made my way towards — I could see her now, bound hand and foot, gagged by a dish-towel —

Not Mrs. Tupper!

"They 'it me!"

Tied to a kitchen chair was a rawboned girl perhaps twelve years old, whose swaddled, wet, and reddened face I did not recognise at first as I cut the twine that secured her feet and hands. But as she herself tore the gag off, I realised that it was Florrie, Mrs. Tupper's daily girl-of-all-work, whom I had seen only a few times, as she generally finished before I arrived home.

Where was Mrs. Tupper?

"They laid 'ands on me!" Florrie spewed forth such a torrent of woe that no sense could be got out of her, while I burned with fear that my landlady lay insensible, or hurt, or — or worse. But I saw no sign of her downstairs. Leaving Florrie to her hysterics, I rushed up to Mrs. Tupper's bedchamber, dagger in hand. But I found only more ruins — bedstead flung aside and everything from the wardrobe and dresser thrown on the floor; not an inch of carpet was to be seen. Such were the heaps of sheets and blankets mixed with shoes, skirts, shawls, and unmentionables that at first I thought Mrs. Tupper might be lying somewhere underneath. Throwing my dagger aside, like a demented badger I burrowed amongst bed linens, penny weeklies, house-dresses, rheumatism cures, aprons and frocks and—and my landlady's old black Sunday bonnet—

Holding the venerable bonnet freshly trimmed with new ribbons for Easter, I felt sick yet calmer, more sane.

I retrieved my dagger and sheathed it, reasoning that if there were brigands still in the house, they would have attacked me by now; also, Florrie would have fled the kitchen, whereas I could still hear her lamentations echoing up the stairs.

Having failed to find Mrs. Tupper in her bedroom, I checked my own. Oddly, it had not been ransacked like the rest of the house. I looked into the wardrobe and under the bed. Mrs. Tupper—or what I dreaded to find, her mortal remains my landlady was not there.

I ran back downstairs. Florrie had moved only to stand up, but her wails were increasingly taking the shape of words. "Gennelmums, my 'ind foot!" Barely intelligible; I could catch a few words now and then. "Come bustin' in 'ere . . . slappin' a respegguble girl . . . 'ouse all sixes an' sevens . . ."

"Where is Mrs. Tupper?" I interrupted.

". . . rat-face curs fit fer the sewer . . ."

I took her by the shoulders. With difficulty I restrained myself from shaking her. "Florrie. Where is Mrs. Tupper?"

". . . an' 'er makin' pudding dough wit' 'er sleeves rolled up, nuttin' on 'er 'ead but 'er 'ouse-cap . . ."

I went ahead and shook the obtuse girl, shouting, "Where is Mrs. Tupper?"

Jerking herself free of my hands, Florrie shouted back at me as if I were the dense one, "I been telling ye! They took 'er!"

It required an excruciating hour for me to get the tale out of Florrie. She would not calm down for any coaxing, and eventually I had to say I would summon a constable. (I could not possibly do so, for I myself was a runaway, wanted by Scotland Yard as well as by my very formidable brothers—but the girl did not know that.) Florrie, like any proper East Ender, dreaded having anything to do with the police, so she sat down in a kitchen chair as I told her to, and tried to talk sensibly. "They was dressed like gents, or I wouldn't 'ave let them in."

"How many?" I had put the kettle on the stove and was trying to find a cup that was not broken so that I could give her tea.

"Two big bearded blokes."

"And what did they look like?"

"They 'ad beards like Anarchists."

And very probably fake. As patiently as I could, I responded, "Aside from the beards. What colour was their hair, for instance?"

She didn't recall.

"How tall?"

She couldn't really say. They had seemed huge.

"How old do you think they might have been?"

One seemed younger than the other, but not so a person would notice. And so on. The poor girl's dim wits were thoroughly addled by her fright.

Understandably so. As far as I could piece together, the two bearded strangers had knocked at the door, asked politely to speak with Mrs. Tupper, and once within the house had quite changed their tone, demanding to be given the message for the Bird.

"*What?*"

"'They kep' on saying she should give 'em what she 'ad for the Bird."

"A Mr. Byrd, perhaps?"

"No mister, no missus, just 'the Bird,' wot they say. Bellering into 'er ear-trumpet they were, 'We know you was a spy for the Bird!'"

CARRIER PIGEON, the mysterious and threatening missive had addressed Mrs. Tupper before instructing her to deliver her BIRD-BRAINED message. She was a bird who was to report to a Bird, then?

Bizarre as it seemed, a pattern did appear to emerge. Otherwise, I might not have believed the ignorant girl-of-all-work still breathlessly babbling:

"'Wot you got fer the Bird,' they kep' yelling at 'er, an' when she toll 'em an' toll 'em she din 'ave nothing, they smacked 'er—"

The blackguards! How could they strike a poor old woman?

"—an' then they smacked me fer interferin'—"

Florrie had tried to intervene? My feelings for the girl warmed immediately.

"—and they tied me up an' commenced 'unting fer it."

"But—for *what*?"

"I dunno, miss, no more'n Mrs. Tupper did. That flummoxed she were, she cried."

"Villains," I muttered, setting a cup of tea in front of the girl.

"Yes, miss. Thank you, miss."

"There's no sugar, I'm afraid. It's all spilled." I paced the ruined room, unable to sit down with her. "So did these dastardly men find what they were looking for?"

The girl took a long sip of tea, which I could not begrudge her, then finally said, "'Ow wud I know, Miss Meshle?"

Confound her! I wanted to snatch her tea away.

Just because she had been tied up with her back to the door, so that she could not see, could she not have *heard* something? As calmly and civilly as I could I inquired, and she reported one of the villains saying they would "take the deaf old bat along an' 'e could ask 'er 'imself."

Who on earth was "'e"?

Evidently the thugs had not found "the message to the Bird."

Who in perdition were *they*?

Was there anything more to be got out of Florrie?

Forcing myself to sit down so as to cease towering over the unfortunate girl, I began my interrogation of her all over again, but with no satisfactory results, other than the additional information that the older kidnapper was missing some teeth. (From this I could conclude that he was not of the very best class in society.) When Florrie—ridiculous but popular name; one seemed to run across Florries everywhere—when the obtuse wench began to cry again, I knew it was time to desist.

"Very well, Florrie." I gave her a shilling. "Run on home, now, tell your mother all about it, and have her spread the word." Indeed I could not have hushed Florrie's mother, a washerwoman, had I tried; her Irish tongue served as a megaphone for the neighbourhood. "Please let it be known"—I held up a pound note to indicate fiduciary inducement—

"that anyone who saw those men take Mrs. Tupper or who knows anything about it should come here and inform me at once."

Still sniffling, Florrie nodded, then scuttled out the door.

CHAPTER
THE
THIRD

AND DIRECTLY AFTER FLORRIE, I WENT OUT
likewise, still in my striped-and-ruffled poplin dress,
my silly little hat and green glass ear-bobs and false
curls, for Miss Meshle was a familiar sight on that
street, and its other inhabitants would not hesitate to
talk with me. Amongst them I hoped to find wit-
nesses to Mrs. Tupper's abduction.

And so I did, in plenty, for a horse-drawn conveyance was a rarity on that narrow stone-paved
lane, and Mrs. Tupper's unexpected visitors had
arrived in a carriage, no less. Many of the neighbourhood loiterers had noticed it.

The "blind" beggar on the corner divulged that
the strangers had arrived in a shiny black brougham
driven by a pursy, florid man, and the horse had
been a bay.

The corner chandler had seen a phaeton with the top up, a coat-of-arms on the door, with a nondescript narrow sort of driver and a black horse that "would've been good for a funeral."

His wife agreed that there was a picture of a white deer or unicorn or something on the vehicle's door, but said it was a barouche with the top up, not a phaeton, and the horse was brown. The driver had been short and stocky, with a pronounced chin.

The greengrocer had seen a black brougham with bright yellow wheels but no coat-of-arms, drawn by a chestnut horse and driven by a tall, puffy-faced man with a red nose, obviously a heavy drinker and very likely Irish.

The pudding-vendor said that a rather shabby grey cab had waited in front of Mrs. Tupper's house, the heavy, dark horse looked "more fit for a plough," and that the driver had one single eyebrow "as thick as thatch" that ran like a roof clear over his nose.

The "lady of the night" on our street, who would also be a "lady of the day" when opportunity offered, said that she had approached the driver while the carriage sat in front of Mrs. Tupper's house, but had been rudely rebuffed. She said he looked much like any other man, two eyes, mouth, nose in the middle. She said the carriage was black with shiny red wheels, no crest, and the horse was roan.

The street urchins said variously that the horse

was black, brown, or red, that the conveyance was a four-wheeler cab, a carriage, or a coach, that the driver was short, tall, fat, thin, old, young; they agreed only that he was unfriendly, throwing no pennies but rather threatening them with his whip.

Regarding any description of the *occupants* of the cab/phaeton/brougham/barouche/carriage/coach, that is to say, the men who had abducted Mrs. Tupper: no one seemed to have seen them getting out of the conveyance and going into the house. Nor had anyone, *anyone,* observed the kidnappers coming out of the house with Mrs. Tupper in hand, or noticed which way they went. Apparently, the neighbourhood's curiosity had been all for their arrival, not for their departure. And by this time, even if anyone *had* told me what they looked like, I would not have believed a word.

Fit to scream with frustration, and nearly despairing, I returned to the house, lest news arrive from Florrie or her mother, or a demand from the abductors, or something of the sort.

Suppertime had long since passed, but I had no thoughts of eating, nor could I bring myself to sit down, rest, and wait. Rather, I paced the ransacked lower room, kicking broken china out of my way and trying to think. Two rough men demanding a message? *We know you were a spy for the Bird.* Mrs. Tupper, a spy? Ludicrous.

What in the name of nonsense could "the Bird" mean?

What message? My understanding seemed as dim as the single candle I carried for light, as day had long since turned to night.

What in the world could Mrs. Tupper have got herself mixed up in? I could not imagine her intentionally withholding from two rough thugs anything that they wanted. Mrs. Tupper, for all her adventures in the Crimea, seemed to me hardly the sort of person to indulge in heroics. I believed that if she had any inkling what the villains wanted, she would have given it to them at once.

Yet, evidently they had left without it, for why else would they have taken her with them? They believed she knew where it was, and they intended for their master or employer—the man I called X, or perhaps the mysterious Bird—to induce her to relinquish it—

It? What was "it"?

The two intruders had plundered the house as if in search of some physical object.

But obviously they had not found it.

Just as obviously Mrs. Tupper knew nothing of it.

Yet—might it nevertheless be here?

When I was a little girl—less than a year ago, that era before Mum took her unannounced leave, but it seemed a distant past, those green sweet-scented countryside days before all this grey London smut—when I was thirteen-going-on-ten instead of fourteen-going-on-thirty, I used to run out into the woods of Ferndell Park, my home, and look for things, anything, just searching. Climbing trees, peering into the crannies of the rocks, pretending there was some treasure to be found. The trove I accumulated had included jay-feathers, yellow-striped snail-shells, someone's garnet earring, plover-eggs, pennies that had turned green, interesting stones that I suspected might contain gems within them—and I suppose I still look for things of value in unlikely places; this has become my life's calling.

Undertaking to search Mrs. Tupper's house, then, I set about the task not only with energy born of desperation but with the keen interest of a lifelong Nosey-Nellie and with a practised eye to note anything unusual, anything at all.

As the mysterious intruders had most rudely strewn Mrs. Tupper's poor belongings, I took the opposite approach: I put things away. Lighting every candle, every lantern and oil-lamp (in outrageous defiance of the usual parsimony of the place), inch by inch I inspected the dwelling and every item therein by replacing each thing where it belonged.

Or, in the case of broken dishes, sweeping up the shards and depositing them in the dust-bin.

Also shattered were the two crockery spaniels who had guarded the ends of the mantel. I inspected their interior surfaces carefully, but saw no sign that anything had been concealed in them.

The contents of Mrs. Tupper's carved memorabilia box lay torn and strewn on the floor. I inspected them as I collected them: my landlady's babyhood record of baptism so old and brittle it had broken into pieces along the folds, equally ancient sepia-toned photographic portraits most likely of family members, a similar one of stiffly-ranked children being promoted from the Sisters of Mercy Ragged School of Hoisington—Mrs. Tupper had done well for one who had made her start in a ragged school!—the wedding photograph I had seen before, her yellowing marriage certificate, the deed to the house, et cetera. From all of this I discovered that Mrs. Tupper's first name was Dinah, but nothing more.

The hour was late, but I could not possibly sleep; I continued working. When I had inspected and tidied the kitchen and parlour to my dissatisfaction, I tore myself a hunk of bread and forced myself to eat it, knowing I needed to safeguard my strength. Then, gnawing the crust, I trudged upstairs to assail Mrs. Tupper's bedroom.

First, and in haste, begrudging the time, I stopped in my own chamber to rid myself of the increasingly annoying corset, bust enhancer, hip regulators, and other paraphernalia of Miss Meshle. With muted relief I shed my buxom fair-haired disguise to be my scrawny self. In my stocking feet, a dressing gown, and my own lank hair and wedge-of-cheese face, I proceeded to my task.

Every drawer of Mrs. Tupper's dresser had been dumped. With lighted candle in hand I inspected that humble item of furniture for any false bottoms where writings or papers might be concealed; I even pulled it away from the wall to look at its back, and I scrutinised each drawer, inside and out, as I replaced it. Nothing.

With a sigh, I then set about picking up clothing from bed and floor. As I folded Mrs. Tupper's poor, dear old-fashioned pantaloons to return them to the dresser, tears ran down my face; imagine, having strange men in one's bedroom laying callous hands upon one's underpinnings! How perfectly dreadful.

My feelings of lachrymose outrage continued as I examined the empty wardrobe, then began to return strewn and rumpled clothing to its hangers therein. Mrs. Tupper was a good, decent woman, I thought as I handled the muslin blouses and woollen skirts, some of them neatly patched, that she wore on weekdays. No doubt she had been wearing blouse, skirt, apron, and ruffled house-cap when she had been snatched away. How distressed she must be, for Mrs. Tupper never let herself be seen upon the street without first exchanging her apron for a starched white "pinner" and her house-cap for a bonnet!

Skirts were for everyday wear; special occasions required dresses, and Mrs. Tupper managed dresses just as she did everything else: with thrift, moderation, and regularity. She owned no more than four. Each spring she put great thought into the purchase of a new, sensible one appropriate to a woman of her age and humble station yet reasonably current in fashion. And each winter she "made over" one of the older dresses, taking it apart, turning its fabric to the unstained side, and altering its cut and trimming to reflect current trends. What was beyond saving she discarded. She did not keep anything out-of-date; she had got rid of her bustle, for instance, within a year after that ridiculous shelf-like dorsal protrusion had gone out of style.

I was a bit surprised, therefore, to find, amongst the other clothing I rescued from the floor, quite an old-fashioned crinoline frock that must have dated back to the times when it was difficult for a fashionable woman to fit the breadth of her skirt through a doorway. Very well made this dress was, with a ruffled peplum, ruffles at the shoulders also, and yards and yards of Prussian blue silk in its vast skirt, which spread full circle in the style of thirty years ago.

Perhaps the thrifty Mrs. Tupper had kept this relic for the sake of the fabric?

But would she not have cut it up and made use of it long before now?

A sentimental memento, then? Her wedding-dress? It was quite fine enough for one.

But no, I had seen Mrs. Tupper's wedding photo, and I did not recognise this dress from it.

So why in Heaven's name, given her stingy habits and her limited wardrobe space, had she preserved this voluminous gown?

And also, I saw to my renewed surprise as I glanced towards the next garment awaiting me on the floor — she had also kept its crinoline!

CHAPTER THE FOURTH

THE GENTLE READER WILL KINDLY UNDERSTAND that I am not attempting to excuse myself, but merely reporting the truth of the matter, when I say that, at that moment, daylight was dawning literally although not, alas, metaphorically. I had been up all night, had grown stupid in consequence, and I looked upon the crinoline without analytical insight, merely girlish bewilderment: no one had worn the abominable things since 1860 or thereabouts, so why did Mrs. Tupper still have one?

Picking up the crinoline, feeling its heft and the scratchy rigour of its linen-and-horsehair fabric, I could quite see that, although now unstarched and much flattened, nevertheless it had been at one time quite formidable, fit to support and flare even the heaviest nine-yards-of-fabric flounced-and-ruffled skirt. Constructed in the form of a tiered petticoat, the crinoline widened enormously from top to bottom, each panel much larger than the last and gathered into it, the seams being covered by sturdy grosgrain ribbon embroidered with flowers.

I found myself gazing at those blossomy embellishments.

Unlike most well-bred young ladies, I had never been taught to embroider. My mother, a Suffragist, had scorned the drawing-room graces, encouraging me to read books, ride my bicycle, wander the woods, and climb trees, not to mould wax roses, string seashells, hem hankies, or bead eyeglass-cases. I knew how to do sensible everyday sewing, of course, such as darning stockings or mending a seam, but not decorative stitchery of any sort.

Perversely, then, I quite admired the crinoline's adornment of blue ribbon embroidered with flowers of pink, peach, yellow, lavender, and other lovely pastel hues, for I thought embroidered posies very pretty indeed and wished I knew how to make them. I had even gone so far as to learn a few basic stitches from the *Girl's Own Paper* — well, only two, actually, French Knot and Lazy Daisy, which I recognised on the crinoline's ribbons. I had never seen embroidered ribbon before, but I would have expected a repeating pattern of some sort; the blue grosgrain, however, was decorated with a sweet and artless sequence, random as to both colour and arrangement, of wild roses and starflowers—quite winsome while simple to achieve, I realised, peering more closely. The starflowers were five Lazy Daisy stitches around a French Knot, and the little roses were nothing more than thread wrapped under and over three crossed stitches—

What ever was I thinking? My poor deaf land-lady missing, kidnapped, maybe injured or even—despatched—and there I stood gawking at *embroidery*?

Thrusting the crinoline into the wardrobe, I continued my search for something that might help explain what had happened to Mrs. Tupper, or give me some clue as to her whereabouts. After putting away her few remaining clothes, I examined her bed as I put it back together, looked under her night-stand and her wash-stand, even studied her stacks of gossip-and-fashion periodicals, but without any helpful results. I even turned up her carpet, and found nothing under it. With a sigh, I sat down on her bed, looking about me and trying to think. I had looked at the floor. I studied the walls. I lay down to scan the plasterwork of the ceiling. . . .

I was awakened only an hour or two later by Flor-rie. "Oh, Miss Meshle," she gasped, "such a turn ye gave me. All the lamps on and no sign of ye downstairs or in yer room — I thought they'd come and got ye, too!"

"What? Who?" I mumbled, unable momentarily to remember where I was or what I was about or even *who* I was. Miss Meshle? I thought my name was Enola Holmes.

"Miss Meshle," said Florrie anxiously, "ye don't look like yerself. Why, ye've lost that much weight overnight wot with worrying about Mrs. Tupper and all, it's a wonder ye're yet alive."

The simple girl had never seen me without my padding, plus the rubber devices I usually stuffed into my mouth and nostrils to fill out the shape of my face. I looked quite different, I am sure, and she thought the change was wrought by Mrs. Tupper's disappearance.

"Now she may well be dead, wot me mother says — "

This jolted me upright. "Florrie, do please hush!" Mrs. Tupper, perished, murdered? Such nonsense — well, perhaps not nonsense — still, it did not bear saying.

Florrie did not hush. " — but the rest of us must go on living, an' if you hain't et something yet, you should 'ave an egg an' a cup of tea straightaway."

What an odd creature the girl was, with her clumsy bony personage and her round childish face. Trying to take care of me, forsooth. I found myself

41

almost smiling as I sat on the edge of my landlady's bed. "Florrie," I asked gently, "is there any news of Mrs. Tupper?"

"I don't know wot you'd rightly call it news, miss, for folk talk of nothin' else, and some says she were taken by Red Anarchists, but others says it's them gangs from the dockyards are to blame, and some even says it's Jack the Ripper." Florrie shivered. "It couldn't be that, could it, miss? Mrs. Tupper were a respegguble woman."

Her use of the past tense, already, jarred me to my feet. "She still is, I hope. You're quite correct, Florrie, I need something to eat so that I can better think what to do." According to Dr. Watson's accounts of my brother Sherlock, starvation and sleeplessness increased the acuity of the great detective's mental processes, but alas—for I begrudged the time—I found that I functioned much better when rested and fed.

"'At's right, miss." Florrie started downstairs.

But as I turned to follow her out of the room, my glance caught on the wardrobe still hanging open, and on its contents.

"Florrie," I called after the girl, "would you happen to know why Mrs. Tupper kept this?" I pulled out the exquisite old-fashioned blue silk dress.

"Oh, yes, miss!" With considerable enthusiasm, Florrie reversed course, running back into the bedroom. "She showed it to me once, miss, because it were given to her by the lady I was named after. Or not me, exactly, bein' I were named after my aunt, but my aunt were named after her."

Confound the babbling girl, she made my head ache. I think I persevered only because there was nothing else to do. "Who?"

"The lady, miss, the one wot gave Mrs. Tupper the dress!"

I took a deep breath. "Start over, Florrie. Slowly, please. Who gave Mrs. Tupper this gown?"

Anxious to please me, Florrie frowned with distress. "I disremember her name exactly, miss, but she were famous at the time. The Lady with the Lamp, they called 'er when Aunt Flo was born, but nobody 'card nothing 'bout 'er fer years now."

Mrs. Tupper had said something about a Lady with a Lamp, hadn't she? With some strain my weary brain began to make connections. Thirty-four years ago, forgotten now. Crimean War. *Fine clothes she give me, better'n what I was married in* — this had to be the mid-century crinoline dress I held in my hands.

"Now, what were that lady's name?" Florrie muttered.

One of those crossword-puzzle names once famous but slowly being forgotten . . . But what could any of this possibly have to do with our immediate and pressing difficulties? "It doesn't matter." I put the dress back into the wardrobe and closed the doors on it. "Come along, Florrie."

The girl obeyed, trailing downstairs after me, but she kept mumbling. "Florence. Florence something," as I slumped in a kitchen chair and she put the kettle on for tea. "Peculiar name, sort of dark. Blackwell? Blackwood? Blackbird?"

Suddenly it came to me. "Florence Nightingale."

"'At's it!" Florrie appeared much relieved. "Night-in-gaol, must've 'ad a scoundrel back o' the family somewheres, but she were a fine lady fer all that—"

"Not Night-in-gaol," I interrupted, forgetting to erase my aristocratic accent, such was my fatigue and irritation. "No slur of imprisonment exists. A nightingale is simply a sweetly singing bird of the thrush family—"

Within my mind I experienced a sensation reminiscent of the flash powder exploding above a portrait photographer's camera, and I rocketed to my feet, nearly upsetting the table. "Ye gods!" I shouted in a most unruly fashion. "The Bird!"

CHAPTER THE FIFTH

THE LADY WITH THE LAMP HERSELF MUST BE deceased by now, I assumed, because any veteran of the Crimean War I had ever met had been tottering on the edge of the grave, and those men had been youths at the time of the conflict, whereas Florence Nightingale had been a middle-aged woman; surely, as I had not heard her name mentioned in years, she had long since passed away. But perhaps some surviving member of the Nightingale family might know something of Mrs. Tupper's history, or even of her present whereabouts? It was a most tenuous clue, but I clutched at it in the proverbial manner, for it was the only straw I had.

After gulping some bread and tea, I ran upstairs to dress, casting about in my mind for the best way in which to present myself. Miss Meshle was too vulgarly working-class to merit respect or receive admission, yet the pristinely upper-class Miss Viola Everseau would take hours to put together, and I had no patience for her; my hands shook as I snatched clothing out of my wardrobe, settling upon a plain and narrow brick-coloured merino dress. In this, with my mud-brown hair in a bun and a pair of tortoiseshell-rimmed spectacles upon my bony face, I would pass as a particular variety of upper-class female, the kind who espouses causes and studies (or attempts to study, when not being harassed by proprietary males) at the British Museum, an unconventional young woman with no interest in marriage, but nevertheless a lady of sorts—even though no lady who aspired to beauty would ever be seen in eyeglasses.

Glancing into the mirror, I quite approved of the glasses, for their heavy dark rims disguised my face, especially the length of my rather alarming nose. I added a slightly mannish black hat. Excellent. I had rendered myself such a free-thinking spinsterish object that no one would take any notice of me. There remained only the matter of jacket and gloves—ink-stained, of course—as I sallied forth, calling, "Florrie, will you stay until I get back?" I wanted her there at the house in case someone came with news.

"Of course, Miss—" She caught sight of me, and her jaw faltered. "Miss, um—Meshle?"

"Never mind, Florrie."

"Ye're going to look fer Mrs. Tupper?"

"Of course, Florrie. But let us hope she makes her way home on her own before too long."

Would that it were to be so.

The streets of the East End brawled as always with unwashed humanity—ragged, half-starved street urchins, a beggar with hideous festering "burns" made of soap scum and vinegar, street vendors bawling "Puddings an' pies!" or "Ginger beer!" or "Fish 'ere! Fresh 'erring!" with voices hoarse from shouting. Walking amidst washerwomen and other sorts of daily help hurrying towards the city, I noticed a tall, muscular workman, his plaid cloth cap rather too large for him, sauntering along; he would be late for his job at that rate.

Once I had passed the Aldgate Pump, a twenty-foot monstrosity topped with a grandiose lamp, I was able to summon a cab, for the monument to Light and Hygiene marked the beginning of a less odiferous, more respectable part of the city. As the cab-driver stopped for me, I told him, "Florence Nightingale School of Nursing."

"Right-o, miss." I settled back into the open seat

of the hansom cab as if I assumed the man knew where I was going, although I myself had no idea; I had heard only that there was such a school somewhere in London.

As we trotted along, I heard my cabbie yell to another one, "'Ey! Whereabouts be the nursie school?"

It turned out to be across London Bridge, on the other side of the Thames, in Lambeth near St. Thomas' Hospital. As I alighted from the cab and paid the driver, I observed—walking the paths of a small formal garden two by two, silently, as if performing a task, in the fine May sunshine—young women wearing starched white collars, aprons, and caps over brown frocks so homely that even my merino seemed handsome by comparison. These, I surmised, were the nurses-in-training.

As they seemed indisposed to speak to me or even to look at me, I made for the massive front door of the sizeable but unlovely brick building, knocked, then saw a small placard directing one to "Walk In," and did so.

Another small sign, with a hand painted upon it pointing the direction, showed me to the office. Within, I found a desiccated-looking matron, dressed in black, who looked me up and down in an appraising manner.

Oh, dear. She thought I was applying to be a

trainee. To my annoyance I found myself babbling with nerves. "I have not come—that is—I'm not, um—I am trying to locate some member of the Nightingale family in regard to a personal matter."

The dried-out woman blinked several times. "Some member?"

"I, um, Miss Florence Nightingale—"

I was trying to say in the most delicate way that surely the famous spinster herself was no longer available to be interviewed—but I spoke no farther, for quite briskly the matron nodded, reaching for a piece of paper. When she had written upon this, she handed it to me.

"Thirty-five South Street," I read aloud, then looked up in astonishment. "Miss Nightingale is *alive*?"

I am sure I looked quite mawkish, for the twiggy matron smiled. "Oh, very much so. Although she does not go out at all."

Oh, dear, it would be scarcely bearable if she were alive but unable to speak with me. "Is she unwell? Or, um, wandering in her mind?"

"Senile? Hardly." The dry stick actually chuckled. "Nor is she often ill. It's mostly that, after coming home from the Crimea and taking to her bed, she simply has not got out again."

"She's, ah, um, she's an invalid?" Bad news, or so I thought, for I knew invalids as peevish, malingering, demanding people who simply chose not to be valid, so to speak. Scarcely a household in upper-class England had not at one time or another suffered under the paradoxical power of the invalid. Many a lady thwarted had taken to her bed for the sake of ordering folk about. Indeed, I had done so myself, for a few weeks after my mother had run away, although in my case it was in order to avoid unpleasantness in general and my brother Mycroft in particular.

But—nearly thirty-five years?

The matron said, "She prefers to be referred to as a valitudinarian. But if invalid she is, then surely she's the most active invalid in London." Then the woman gestured dismissal as if I were no more than a child. "Run along, dear. It's time for me to call the probationers in from their constitutional."

Out I went, my mind rife with perturbing thoughts of the heroic Florence Nightingale now recumbent. Here lay yet another statue with feet of clay, I brooded. Would the erstwhile "Lady with the Lamp" shed any light at all upon the darkness surrounding the fate of Mrs. Tupper?

Lambeth was an orderly sort of place, with not many people on the street at this mid-morning hour. Somewhat to my surprise, I noticed that one of the passersby was the same sauntering workman in an overlarge plaid hat whom I had seen in the East End earlier. Perhaps he was employed hereabouts?

Finding a cab-stand, I got into another hansom and told the driver, "Thirty-five South Street."

But rather than starting off at once, he exclaimed, "In *Mayfair*, miss?"

My surprise was scarcely less than his, but I hope I concealed it. "Is that where South Street is?"

"Yes, miss."

"Then let us go there."

Small wonder he had checked to see whether he had heard me rightly, for Mayfair is London's most exclusive neighbourhood. One would expect a woman who has martyred her life for humanitarian causes to live — I don't know where, but not in May-fair, with the wealthy and powerful. Was Florence Nightingale rich? I supposed, now that I thought about it, she must have had considerable means in order to do the remarkable things she had done. But why, if she was born into a wealthy family, the sort to be presented at court, had she gone instead to a bloody cesspool of a hospital in the Crimea? And why now, confining herself to bed, did she live amongst courtiers? Jouncing along in the cab, I entertained a doubtful yet lively curiosity regarding Florence Nightingale.

No amount of thought and speculation, however,

could have prepared me for what I found at 35 South Street, just off Park Lane—indeed, the house was so situated as to enjoy a view of Hyde Park! And a worthy house it was, a large, handsome four-storey brick edifice, its area enclosed in wrought-iron railings, its shutters and trimmings painted a rich and restrained green.

After taking several deep breaths, I climbed stone steps to a stately door with fan-light. I plied a polished brass knocker, quite expecting to be met by a suitably fearsome butler who would question me, then usher me into a hushed, deep-carpeted library or parlour where I would wait alone for a considerable period of time before—

The door opened, and a young man who was neither a butler nor a footman, but wore an exceedingly fashionable tweed suit with knickerbockers and tall tan gaiters, stood aside with hardly a glance at me and said, "Come in."

And from the doorstep I smelled the mingled aromas of tea, pastries, and cut flowers, while I heard the babble of many voices.

"I beg your pardon," I said, put rather off balance, "am I interrupting something?"

"Not at all." He barked a short laugh. "It's like this every day of the week. Do come in."

Sensing impatience in his voice, I did as he said, stepping into a broad, well-lit hallway off of which opened parlour, library, morning-room, dining-room, and so on, several spacious rooms, and in every one of them sat men in city-suits and women in visiting-dresses either chatting, or taking tea, or poring over documents, or writing, or any combination of the above. With quite a shock to my already-fuddled mind I recognised erstwhile Prime Minister Gladstone amongst the crowd.

I began to realise that my obtaining even a few moments of Miss Nightingale's undivided attention might present considerable difficulty.

CHAPTER
THE
SIXTH

LIKE A SHIP BECALMED, I DRIFTED UPON THE SISAL carpet just inside the door, for the young man who had admitted me was now nowhere to be seen, and I did not know how to proceed. Baffled, I studied the furnishings of the passageway: ingenious yet attractive settees that incorporated hat-racks, mirrors, and umbrella-stands into their construction, a towering casement-clock, cabinets displaying memorabilia presumably from the Crimea, embroidered mottoes framed to hang on the walls: *Patience and Persistence Prevail, Good Intentions Cannot Mend Bad Sense, Without Progress We Regress*, that sort of thing, daintily stitched with borders of flowers.

As I studied *Without Progress We Regress* thoughtfully, a silk-gowned young woman, certainly not a servant, sailed past me with a pitcher of lemonade and some glasses on a tray. Although there certainly were no wasps to be fended off so early in the year, still, the pitcher was draped with a delicately daisy-broidered jug cover. So taken was I with this lovely object that I rather startled when the young lady paused to ask me in the friendly manner of an equal, "Are you here in regard to hospital reform, miss?"

Despite my pose of womanhood, I found myself replying like the callow fourteen-year-old girl I was. "Um, no . . ."

"Or concerning the deplorable conditions in our workhouses?"

I shook my head.

"You are not on the Army Medical Commission, surely." Cheerfully the young lady continued her attempt to place me. "The Committee for the Licensing of Trained Nurses?"

Like a stupid child I shook my head, but then managed to say, "I need to ask Miss Florence Nightingale a question."

"That's easily arranged. See Mrs. Crowley at the desk in the library," she told me with a nod and a smile.

Mrs. Crowley, a somewhat older version of the richly gowned young lady who had directed me to her, also smiled and nodded as I said I wanted to speak to Florence Nightingale. She did not ask my name, luckily for me, as I had no idea what it might be today. Nor did she request a card to be sent up to the invalid, or a letter of introduction. Quite without questioning my intrusion in any way, she merely waved me to a nearby seat and handed me a laptop writing-desk complete with pen, ink, and a sheaf of cream-coloured rag paper of the very best quality.

I regarded this array with such evident bewilderment that Mrs. Crowley told me gently, "Write down what it is you wish to ask Miss Nightingale, and that young jackanapes in the knickerbockers will take it up to her, and as soon as she has time, she will write you a reply."

Baffled, I stammered, "But—but I really need to speak directly with Miss Nightingale!"

Mrs. Crowley's smile widened slightly. "Oh, no, I see you do not understand that is quite impossible," she told me with only the kindliest hint of reproach in her voice. "No one speaks *directly* with Miss Nightingale." Benignly Mrs. Crowley nodded towards a doorway across the hall, through which was visible the imposing form of Mr. Gladstone. "If His Excellency wishes to ask her something, he sends up a note. They all do."

"But—but if she is such an invalid, how can she—"

"It is astonishing how much she accomplishes from her bed, dear. She takes her meals alone, and works constantly. In addition to household notes, she writes sometimes as many as one hundred letters a day, being instrumental in a great many reforms, although she never allows her name to be mentioned in the press. Amongst those in the know, however, the saying is that there are really three, not merely two, Houses of Parliament, and they are the House of Lords, the House of Commons, and the House of Florence Nightingale."

I believe I said rather weakly, "Good heavens. I had no idea. Nevertheless, I really do need to see Miss Nightingale in person —"

"It is simply not possible." Mrs. Crowley began to sound the slightest bit tart. "You appear to be a scholar; you *do* know how to write, don't you?"

"But this may be a matter of life or death!"

Utterly unimpressed, Mrs. Crowley remarked, "Miss Nightingale would not see her parents when they were alive, nor her sister, nor, with few exceptions, anyone else in the past thirty years, so I think it unlikely that she will see you. But you can of course ask." With a gesture of finality, she indicated the writing implements in my lap.

Confound everything, if there had been any ivy on the walls of this most peculiar house, I would have gone outside and attempted to climb it to the reclusive Miss Nightingale's chamber. As there was none, however, I scowled at the paper set before me.

Even though I felt certain the effort was of no avail, eventually I wrote,

Dear Miss Nightingale,
Time is pressing; I will be direct: an elderly woman has been abducted by brigands, seemingly because she knew you in the Crimea and carried a message for you. Her name is Mrs. Dinah Tupper. Have you any idea where she might be, or who has taken her?

A Friend

After blotting and folding this, I handed it to the ever-smiling Mrs. Crowley, who took it with a nod and offered the hospitality of the house with a gesture. "Have some tea, dear, or some lemonade, and biscuits. You will be informed the moment you receive a reply."

This Miss Nightingale certainly did carry the tyranny of invalidism to an extreme. I pictured her as a thoroughly petulant woman, and although I quite felt as if I wanted to strangle—if not her, then at least something or someone—still, I managed a meek enough nod as I got up and ambled off.

While attempting to appear purposeless, actually I had become keenly interested in certain aspects of the interior of this house.

Wandering through the rooms of the ground floor, past tables where numerous visitors partook of finger sandwiches, sliced fruit, hot pastries, and the like—Miss Nightingale certainly gave freely of every hospitality except her own presence!—I eyed embroidered napkins, embroidered table-linens and seat-cushions, even embroidered jam-pot covers! The latter were cunningly stitched with depictions of raspberries, grapes, peaches, apricots, strawberries, currants, or quinces, forsooth, to match the flavours of the preserves they protected.

Certainly one might expect to find plentiful samples of the ladylike art of embroidery in any upper-class house. Yet I saw no other ladylike arts such as moulded wax flowers, or homemade ruffled silk lamp-shades, or useless little boxes put together out of seashells, or hand-painted glassware, now, did I? Passing into the front parlour, I found no fillet-crocheted antimacassars, but numerous lovingly embroidered pillows. On the walls I saw framed embroidery landscapes as well as the usual plethora of family portraits, some painted, some photographic, a few old-fashioned black-paper silhouettes.

I gave my attention to the photographic prints—various handsome head studies, some of them in profile like the silhouettes; also some full-length wedding portraits, and a few less formally posed—an old man and a remarkably plain younger woman relaxing in the stonework doorway of a country house, a different old man and a different unlovely woman taking tea at a garden table. I was attempting to guess at relationships when the fashion-plate young "jackanapes in the knickerbockers" came to find me, offering me a note that was, one might assume, my answer from the unapproachable Miss Nightingale. In delicate violet-hued ink on thin violet-scented paper, it quite contrasted with the missive I had sent upstairs.

I took it, but before reading it, I gestured towards the portraits on the wall and asked the young man, "Would you be so good—can you tell me who these people are?"

"Oh! Most of them, I can't say, I'm afraid, but those"—he indicated the old couple at the garden table—"are William Edward Nightingale and Fanny Smith Nightingale, Miss Florence Nightingale's parents. And that"—the rather toad-faced young woman in the stone doorway—"is Miss Frances Parthenope

Nightingale, taken at Embley, the family home. Miss Parthe, as she generally is called, is Miss Florence Nightingale's older sister."

Scanning the ranks of portraits for a similar toad-like visage, I asked, "Which of these might be Miss Florence Nightingale?"

"None of them. She dislikes to have her likeness taken or displayed."

Small wonder, if she resembled her sister.

And if she was so ill-favoured, small wonder that she had remained a spinster and had become — bitter? A nearly total recluse, in any event, even from her own family.

After the tweedy young man had gone off again, I looked at the violet-scented note. Written in small and very correct handwriting rather like that of a bookkeeper, it said:

I regret that I cannot help you, knowing no one by the surname of Tupper, nor anything of the matter which perplexes you. I am sorry.

Sincerely,
Florence Nightingale

And that was that.

Except, of course, that it couldn't be. I would not allow it to be.

But I left the house willingly and quietly enough,

for several intriguing thoughts occupied my mind, thus:

Someone in that house quite liked to embroider.

Although no one, to my knowledge, had made a study of the subject, or written a monograph (as my brother Sherlock, for instance, was wont to write monographs upon cigar-ash, ciphers, and chemical reactions), still, it seemed reasonable to hypothesise that embroidery, like handwriting, might vary from individual to individual: dainty or bold, elongated or round, tight or loose, regular or irregular, depending on the stitcher.

The embroidery in Florence Nightingale's house had a certain winsome, airy simplicity, and I had seen quite similar embroidery before.

On the ribbons of a crinoline.

Now, this was odd. Ribbon was an expensive decoration. Embroidery was a labourious decoration. One or the other was generally considered enough; combining the two was an extravagance worthy of a wedding-gown.

Why, then, lavish such effort upon a *crinoline*? The roughest and ugliest of underpinnings? Never to be seen, not even by a bridegroom upon his wedding night?

Altogether, I felt quite eager to get home and have another look at that humble garment.

Chapter the Seventh

Hired transportation was plentiful along Park Lane. "Cab!" I hailed with one gloved hand uplifted.

"Cab!" similarly hailed a gentleman who happened to be walking behind me, and he strode past me to take the next four-wheeler after mine.

Idly watching as he went by, I stiffened as if I had been struck. Which, in a way, I had. By recognition. I had seen this man twice today already, but he had not been a gentleman then. This tall, broad-shouldered fellow had the accent of a gentleman and the bearing of a gentleman — of course; that was why my eye, if not my conscious mind, had noticed him amongst the East End crowd! He had not looked quite right, because a common workman does not saunter along with one hand tucked into his belt behind his back, head up as if he has never borne a burden. Indeed, this self-assured fellow belonged here in the Hyde Park neighbourhood. He had got rid of the rough leather belt around the outside of his jacket, and he had replaced his ridiculous plaid cap with a bowler hat, so that anyone who did not study his boots would take him for a well-to-do merchant in a sack-suit.

Entering my own cab swiftly and applying myself to the window, I got my first good look at his face—a remarkable one. This man's features, while perfectly symmetrical, were pleasantly blunt, not sharp and bony like those of most aristocrats. Artistically speaking, his profile was a model of correct proportion, causing some elusive recognition to niggle at me; where had I seen it before?

But my main concern at the time was, what to do about him?

My cab had driven scarcely a block when I reached a decision. Thumping with my fist at the interior of the roof, I signalled my cab to halt.

Exiting, I told the driver blandly, with no explanation, "Thank you, my good man," paying him a full fare. Then I walked back the way I had come. The other cab, hired by the man who was following me, had pulled up behind mine, naturally enough. With the corner of one eye I saw Classic Profile, as

I was beginning to call him, studiously turned towards the far window as I walked past.

When I came to a girl selling posies, I paused to buy myself a nosegay of lily-of-the-valley, for two purposes: to show reason for my sudden apparent change of mind, thereby calming any alarm in my adversary, and also in order to turn and have a look at his whereabouts. I saw that, while my cabbie had of course driven on to find another fare, Classic Profile's cab remained, as I had hoped, where it was.

Smiling, with my posy to my face as if I were enjoying its fragrance, I walked on a bit farther, then hailed another four-wheeler.

Paying him in advance "for my own convenience," as I vaguely explained, I told him to take me to the British Museum, then stepped in. But just as he slapped his horse with the reins, I stepped out again, by the door on the other side, the street side. Keeping my cab, now rolling away from me, between myself and the observer whom I considered would be most interested, I retreated behind somebody's parked carriage to watch.

As my now-empty cab proceeded down the street, the one occupied by Classic Profile fell in behind it to follow it out of sight.

I admit that I then congratulated myself upon my own cleverness.

For a few moments. Until my own more-severe self squelched me. *Enola, that is quite enough. What have you accomplished? Evidently the fellow knows where you live, as he followed you from the East End this morning.*

I had gained a little time, that was all, and in order to use it, I hurried home.

"Not a word of 'er, Miss Meshle," Florrie replied to my inquiry concerning Mrs. Tupper. Wringing her hands, the gawky girl cracked her protuberant knuckles most provokingly. To distract her, I handed her my nosegay as I rid myself of hat and gloves.

Then with no preamble I showed her what I had prepared for that purpose: in the cab on the way home, using the paper and pencil I always carry along with other essential supplies in my bust en- hancer, I had made several drawings of the mysteri- ous gentleman who had followed me. I had portrayed him with cap, without cap, full face, profile, et cet- era. While only crudely talented as an artist, I do have a knack for "capturing" faces in an exaggerated way, especially when I am feeling a bit wrought.

Which I was. Feeling wrought. Quite. What *ever* might be happening to my poor deaf landlady?

"''At's *'im*!" Florrie shrieked immediately. "The young one wit' the good teeth! 'E hain't got no beard but 'at's 'im just the same, wot took Mrs. Tupper!"

"Along with the other villain." I wanted to make sure her story was not changing. "An older man with bad teeth."

"Yes'm!"

"And it was the older, rougher brute of the two who hit you?"

"No! No, Miss Meshle!" Florrie had the strong hands of a lifelong labourer, yet her finger shook as she pointed at my drawings of the bland-faced youth I called Classic Profile. "It were 'im! 'Im 'oo slapped me an' Mrs. Tupper!"

He had struck a poor old woman?

Good heavens! But to look at him, one would think he was a perfect gentleman. I felt a chill crawl like a serpent down my spine as I realised: What sort of person hid behind his pleasant face?

Still stabbing her big finger at my sketches, Florrie exclaimed, "'Owever'd ye get a hold of 'is picture, Miss Meshle?"

I did not reply, for already the girl knew far too much of me; I would certainly not tell her that I had drawn the likenesses myself.

"Florrie, lock the doors and don't let anyone in without consulting me first," I called over my shoulder as I ran upstairs, for I had urgent business there.

A few moments later, with the stiff and scratchy bulk of Mrs. Tupper's antique crinoline nearly smothering me, I sat beside the window in my room so that I could examine the irksome thing in the light.

Hmm.

All my emotions funneled into a focussed intensity of interest as I studied the blue ribbons embroidered with flowers. First of all, I noticed that said ribbons were not sewn to the crinoline firmly so as to cover its seams, but merely basted lightly in place, as if meant to be removed.

They had been stuck to the crinoline, I surmised, in order to be transported in secrecy to a destination? But why had they been placed on such an ugly—

"Of course," I whispered as the answer dawned on me. "A crinoline does not need to be *washed.*" Whereas petticoats or any other feminine underpinning might be entrusted to servants and washerwomen, perhaps to be stolen or lost, a crinoline need never leave the possession of its wearer.

"How very clever," I murmured, my respect for Florence Nightingale's intelligence increasing by the moment. To encode the trimmings of women's unmentionables—this *had* to be her idea, sprung from a brilliant feminine mind that knew no man would look twice at embroidered ribbon. The two louts who had searched the house had missed it entirely. Even my brother Sherlock, I expected, might have done no better. Heavens, I had nearly overlooked it myself.

With such admiration I scanned the—the cryptograms, for so one might as well call the simple flowers embroidered upon the ribbons.

The gentle reader will perhaps recall that these were starflowers and little round roses in quite a variety of colours—pink, red, yellow, peach, lavender, white, violet, many more—occasionally interspersed with green leaves. I tried first to see whether I could discern any pattern in the use of colour, and in order to do so, I got out my scissors and detached the ribbons from the crinoline—they were, as I have said, merely basted on, quite simple to remove. The denuded crinoline I tossed into a corner, where it stood upon its own folds, a gauzy white presence, like a ghost of Mrs. Tupper.

Quickly dismissing this unfortunate thought—one must not lose hope!—I took the ribbons and placed them in order from top to bottom of the crinoline, that is to say, from shortest to longest, by laying them out upon my bed.

Arranged that way, they reminded me of lines of print. Indeed, I thought, the varied colours of the embroidery might be of no significance except to serve as a blind, to keep the casual observer from noticing that the flowers themselves were not nearly so varied.

Five Lazy Daisy petals; the simplest of star-flowers.

And a few whipped stitches; the smallest, simplest of roses.

And leaves.

And, occasionally, spaces of blue ribbon untouched.

It was the spaces that truly decided me. Why on earth would anyone leave *spaces* if decorating ribbon with embroidery? The odd display before me simply had to be a code.

But how in the world could letters, words, sentences be encoded with only three symbols: star-flower, rose, and leaf or, occasionally, double leaf?

Because my leaden head rebelled at the task before me, I forced myself to think on paper, as I often do, transcribing the embroidered message as symbols. Composing this account upon a type-writing machine as I am now doing, I can achieve much the same effect by using an asterisk to designate a star-flower, a period to designate a miniature rose, and a slash to designate a leaf. Couched in this way, the message read:

. . . . / . * / . . . * / . \/ . * * . /. * . / *
* * / * * * / . . * . \/ . * * / . * . / . / . .
* . / * * * /. * . / * . . \/ . . . / . / . * .
. / . * . . / . . / * . / * * . \/ . . . / . . *

```
/ . * * . / . * * . / . * . . / . . / . / . / . . .
V * . * . / * * * / * . / . . . / * / . * / * .
/ * / . . / * . / * * * / . * * . / . * . . / .
V * * / . * / . * . / * . * / . / * V . * / .
* * . / . * * . / . / . * / . * . . / . / * . .
V * . * . / . * . / . . * / . . / * . * / . . . /
. . . . / . * / * . / * . * / . . . V . . . . /
. * / . * . . / . * . . V . * . / . * / * * . /
. * . . / . * / * . V * . / * * * V . * / . .
. * / . * / . . / . * . . V * * * / . . * . / .
. * . / . . / * . * . / . / . * . / . . . V * . *
. / . * / . * . . / . * . . / * * * / . . * / . .
. V * * * / . * . V . * * / * * * / . * . / .
. . / . V . * * . / . * . / * * * / . . * . / .
. / * / * / . . / * . / * * . V . * * / . . . .
/ . . / . * . . / . V * * / . / * . V . . * .
/ . * . / . / . / * * . . / . V . . . / * / . * /
. * . / . . . * / . V * . . / . . / . V * . . .
/ . / * * . V * . * * / * * * / . . * V . . *
/ . . . / . V . . / * . / . . * . / . * . . / . . *
/ . / * . / * . * . / . V . . . * / . * . V *
. . / . / . . . / . * * . / . * / . . / . * . / .
. / * . / * * . V . . * . / * . V
```

How very elucidating.

(I hope that the kind reader recognises this as a despairing attempt at humour.)

I stared until my eyelids drooped—it must be remembered that I had by this time gone twenty-several hours with very little sleep or food—but my mind, normally nimble, remained inert.

Well, I thought finally, the placement of the double leaf at the end suggested that it might signal the completion of—what? A word? A sentence?

And the single leaf?

Perhaps another sort of divider—but that left only star and dot (as I had hazily begun to label the daisy and rose), and how could any message be conveyed in a mere two symbols?

Surely I must be missing something. The colours in the embroidery? The French knots? What if there were some variation in the French knots at the centres of the starflowers? Paper in hand, I got up and lurched to my bed where the ribbons still lay, bending over to peer at the tiny stitches by quite inadequate candlelight, for by now night had fallen.

Without conscious volition I did likewise, falling onto the bed, and asleep, all in a moment, still fully dressed and with . . * / . et cetera still in hand.

CHAPTER
THE
EIGHTH

I suppose Florrie must have come in before she went home, and, seeing the state of affairs and not wanting to disturb me, she had blown out the candles for the sake of safety. This to explain why, sometime during the night, I awoke to total darkness.

It was my complaining personage that awoke me, my middle regions knotted in such spasms of hunger as to veto sleep. Groaning, trying to remember who I was and what I was about, I sat up on my bed.

Then stiffened.

Something other than myself was groaning.

The house. Stealthy and frightening noises issued from it. There. CREAK.

Someone was creeping up the stairs.

Danger! cried my every nerve, for never had

those steps complained so beneath Mrs. Tupper's slight weight. I heard another creak as another person stepped on the same cantankerous board. There were two intruders; I could hear their footsteps as they felt their way upstairs in the dark.

It is amazing how quickly one's wits, however weary, can react when sufficiently stimulated by terror. Instantly, and as silently as possible, I raked together with my fingers all the ribbons and papers that had lain along with my personage atop the counterpane of my bed. With this precious evidence in hand, I let myself softly down to the floor on the far side of the bed from the door of my chamber.

Just as I heard the turning of the knob, I crouched flat. Just as my door opened.

From my hiding place I could discern the spectral glimmer of a rushlight. I concentrated on remaining still, trying not even to breathe, as the intruders looked in.

"Bed's still made up," one of them said out loud, his deep voice giving evidence of Cockney origins. "Lodger flew the coop, by the looks of things."

"Afraid of kidnappers, and very sensibly so," said the other dryly. His accent, aristocratic in contrast to the first speaker's, and his tenor voice seemed to match those of the man I had heard hailing a cab along Park Lane. "Well, as she's not here, let's have a couple of candles, shall we?"

They helped themselves to two of mine, lighting them with my matches, then exited the room, closing the door behind them.

I breathed out. Then, quickly but as noiselessly as possible, I got up from the floor, slipping off my shoes and laying them on the bed. Stocking-footed, I tiptoed to the door and listened.

They were in Mrs. Tupper's chamber.

". . . blue silk, with the big skirt such as my grandmother used to wear," the aristocratic one was saying in languid, faintly humourous tones, as if he were amused to find himself rummaging a poor old woman's wardrobe. "This ought to be it."

"Oughter, all right. Lemme slit the bottom open."

For a considerable period of time (as befit the considerable circumference of the skirt's hem) I heard the sounds of fabric being ripped by a knife. Slowly and softly at first but with increasing volume and variety, the man began to curse.

"Nuttin'!" he roared in summation.

"Nothing," the other agreed, sounding more amused than otherwise. "The Grand Pooh-Bah will not be pleased. Did the carrier pigeon say it was in the hem?"

"The old lady? She's no right pigeon, don't know nuttin', deaf as a potato, no sense to be got out of 'er. Bird gave 'er a dress is all we found out."

"Well, might there be a paper or something hidden in these ruffles?"

More tearing sounds—that poor, ravaged dress! Mrs. Tupper had certainly been alive when she spoke of it to "the Grand Pooh-Bah," whoever he might be, and that thought lightened my heart—but what might be happening to her?

"Nuttin'," complained the thug again with an oath. "His Lordship is gonna say we cheesed it!"

At the time I thought that "His Lordship" was just another way they referred to the mysterious Mr. X, their leader, who seemed little loved by them.

The aristocratic voice had become bored. "Well, let's take the dress back with us, shall we, and he can have a look for himself."

"Right buffoons we'll look, toting a blithering dress around!" the other grumbled.

"Well, you didn't mind toting a blithering dress when the old lady was still inside it."

"'At's different."

"In broad daylight."

"Well, 'oo was to see us?"

"And who's to see us now except drunks and hussies?" the other retorted as their footsteps strode towards me, passing my door and heading downstairs.

I, for one, I thought, easing the door open a crack to catch a glimpse of them against the streetlit stairwell window. They passed it like shadow-puppets in a play, in profile, although one made small impression on me, for I recognised the other all too well — Classic Profile — and perversely, in that tense moment, my mind chose to remember where I had seen that silhouette before. I very nearly exclaimed aloud; good sense intervened just in time to keep me silent.

I did not, however, possess sufficient good sense to keep me where I was, in safety — not when there was a chance that, by following these men, I might find Mrs. Tupper.

The moment I heard them leave the house, I sprang into motion, pattering stocking-footed down the stairs and dashing to the door, opening it a crack to peep out. As the younger of the two intruders had implied, there was no traffic in the street at this time of night, but right in front of Mrs. Tupper's humble abode waited a carriage, and even in the uncertain light of street-lamps and head-lamps, I could tell that it *was* a very nice little brougham, drawn by a slender hackney horse, and the wheels had yellow spokes. I saw no crest, but that did not mean there was none, for the door stood in shadow. For the same reason I could make little of the two men climbing in.

But my mission was not merely to spy. The moment they had closed themselves into the brougham,

I shot out of Mrs. Tupper's house, trusting and indeed praying that they did not look behind them.

In fictional accounts of derring-do, you see, the hero quite frequently hangs on to the back of a carriage and, enduring agonising cold, pain, or other rigours of personage, yet unperceived by the villains within, is eventually carried to the place where his lady-love is imprisoned.

Determined that Mrs. Tupper deserved no less of me, lifting my skirt—long skirts are a confounded nuisance when one needs to take action—I ran my fastest. The brougham rolled away, for the driver had started the horse, but that amiable creature had not yet broken into a trot when I flung myself at the back of the carriage—the rattling of its metal-sheathed wheels over ruts and stones serving, I hoped, to mask my impact—and swarmed up as if it were quite a wide tree I had to climb.

There like one of Darwin's primates I clung.

But there was nothing by which to hold on! My feet and fingers searched in vain for any projection or indentation, any ledge or luggage-rack which I might grip. Had I thought about it beforehand, I would have known I'd find none, for had the manufacturers of cabs and carriages put such accommodations on the backs of them, every street urchin and loiterer in London would have been availing himself of free transportation—but such thoughts came to me too late. Splayed like an over-large dark spider on far too smooth a wall, I felt myself being dislodged a little more with the brougham's every jounce.

Indeed, within less than a block I fell off, landing without dignity upon my posterior. My chagrin, as I sat in the filth of the street and watched the brougham roll away from me, can scarcely be described.

Ignoring several laughing "drunks and hussies," in an exceedingly foul mood I got up and stalked home.

I spent what remained of the night forcing my outraged personage to accept some bread and cheese, having a wash, changing my dress for a similarly austere and scholarly costume of brown, then finally, at daylight, sitting down to struggle once again with the puzzle presented to me by the cryptic crinoline. But to no avail; dots and daisies made no sense to me.

I did, however, have one small remaining clue to pursue.

The earliest possible polite hour for social calling found me upon Florence Nightingale's doorstep in Mayfair. This time it was the silk-gowned girl who admitted me without demur; apparently just about anyone could simply walk in here. Even at nine in the morning, I saw and heard as I entered, the drawing-room, dining-room, library, and so forth were well populated with visitors partaking of tea and scones, and already I saw "that young jackanapes" running upstairs with a note from somebody.

What a very odd household.

But I need not stay long today, I hoped. Straight-away I took myself to the front parlour—unpeopled during breakfast—where the walls were covered with portraits either painted, photographic, or scis-sored with exquisite precision from black paper, such being the venerable art of the silhouette.

I found the silhouette I recognised and looked up at it again. Most such cut-paper creations, like the upper-class beings they represent, tend to be a bit grotesque—all nose, or all chin, or both—but this one displayed perfectly proportioned, exceedingly pleasant features. And how often really *does* one see such classic symmetry? Yes, if it were at all possible to identify a person merely from his profile, I was about to do so.

Small, as were most silhouettes, the artwork hung above my reach. Gathering resolve by thinking of poor Mrs. Tupper, wherever she might be, boldly I betook myself to the dining-room, picked up a chair, and walked off with it. As I had hoped, in this pecu-liar house no one seemed to wonder what I was doing.

Positioning the chair, then clambering up to stand

upon it, I lifted the silhouette off its hook. Climbing down again and sitting on the chair that had served as my stool, I turned my find over.

Yes. Yes, it was as I had hoped. On the brown paper backing of the frame, someone had pencilled the subject's name.

It read, *The Honourable Sidney Whimbrel, at Embley, Summer 1853.*

1853?

Thirty-six years ago?

This could not be my aristocratic villain after all. How very disappointing.

Where *was* Classic Profile today? I had not seen him following me at all. Of course, if he was thinking of me merely as Mrs. Tupper's interfering lodger, having now concluded that I had fled to lodge elsewhere, he might have no further interest in me.

Whatever his original interest might have been.

And whoever he was.

So much for my ideas of identifying a person by means of a silhouette.

Sighing, I arose to return it to its place upon the wall, but just at that moment a group of chatting persons entered the parlour, and I lost my nerve, slipping the silhouette into an old leather satchel I had with me today, the sort of case in which a student might carry papers. I, however—as the capacity of my bust enhancer had limits—was using it to carry things I felt it would be unwise to leave behind at Mrs. Tupper's house. Certain ribbons, for instance.

Exiting the parlour, I found myself facing the library, where the smiling yet redoubtable Mrs. Crowley held sway behind her desk.

It could do no harm, I realised, to have another go at Florence Nightingale, asking to speak with her. Indeed, I saw no other course of action before me. Yet I felt defeated in advance, as if no possible eloquence of mine could wring the favour of an interview from the Lady with the Lamp on high, and I experienced a leaden reluctance as I walked into the library in order to speak with Mrs. Crowley, compose a note, have it sent upstairs—

Blast and confound everything! Confound especially Florence Nightingale! What an utterly coddled, perverse, and cantankerous bossy-boots she must be! Her cumbersome procedure of communicating via the passing of notes was a culpable waste of time. If the woman had the means she seemed to possess, and if she insisted on being such a stubborn invalid that she could not be spoken with, yet kept her fingers inserted into so many reform-political pies, why, then, she should jolly well arrange to have notes whisked upstairs on little wires—or, no, she should make use of pneumatic tubes like the ones in shopping emporiums. Or, better yet—the absurdity of this thought offered me dark amusement—she should have a telegraph system installed. If Florence Nightingale insisted on lolling in her bed and sending messages downstairs as if from a great distance, why then, she should tap them out for a teletype machine, dit dit dah dah dit —

A shock of revelation appropriately electric in nature coursed through me, jolting me to a halt. "Ye gods in holey stockings," I cried out loud. "Morse code!"

CHAPTER THE NINTH

UNDERSTANDABLY, NUMEROUS HEADS TURNED. Doing my best to ignore them, with feverish haste, as befit the heat in my cheeks, I made towards the opposite wall of the library, where I spied upon the shelves the unmistakable stately ranks of the *Encyclopaedia Britannica*. Seizing volume *M*, I seated myself at the nearest table—the people already there edged away from me, giving me plenty of room. With trembling hands I found the page:

"International Morse Code uses short and long sounds, which are written out as dots and dashes."

Yes! Already, instinctively, I thought of the miniature roses as dots. The daisies—very rudimentary blossoms of five petals; starflowers—had to be the dashes. Grabbing . . . . / . * / . . . * / . ∨ et cetera from my satchel and referring to the chart in the encyclopaedia (which the gentle reader will find reproduced at the end of this book for the sake of education and amusement), I began to decode — no simple process, as I had to scan the entire alphabet in search of each letter.

Four dots — H. A leaf to divide it from the next letter. Dot, dash — A. Another leaf. Dot, dot, dot, dash — V. Leaf. Single dot — E. Two leaves?

End of word!

HAVE. *Have!*

Quite a while later I had decoded the first five words — HAVE PROOF WREFORD SELLING SUPPLIES — but the bulk of the message remained before me, and I faced a decision: to sit here spending more hours doing this, while Heaven only knew what might be happening to Mrs. Tupper, or to speak with Florence Nightingale at once? For I considered that I now knew how to achieve this seemingly impossible feat.

Deciding on the latter, then, I returned my papers and pencil to their satchel and approached the formidable Mrs. Crowley at her desk. This time, when I asked to speak with Florence Nightingale and she handed me the portable desk with its creamy paper and dark blue ink, I smiled and accepted it without demur.

It cannot with accuracy be said that I wrote upon the paper; rather, I penned. Or drew. Quite quickly and simply I traced:

❁ ❁ ❁ ⬭ ✳ ✳ ✳ ⬭ ❁ ❁ ❁ ⬭ ⬭

Blotting, then folding this short and unsigned missive, I handed it over, and, as the young fellow in knickerbockers took it up, I went and stood at the bottom of the stairs.

In less than a minute, Jackanapes (as I had come to think of him) trotted down again with quite a startled look on his face to tell me, "Miss Nightingale says she will see you. Follow me, please."

My every inference concerning the remarkable Florence Nightingale proved wrong, as became apparent to me within a few minutes. At the very top of the house, in a spacious chamber awash with light from undraped windows, she awaited me: a plump, sweet, smiling old-fashioned beauty sitting up in a large bed richly and tidily arrayed with ribbon-edged pillows and silky eiderdown "puff." Her hair, parted in the centre and smoothed back in the simple manner of her youth, had not yet turned grey! Her lovely, symmetrical face showed scarcely a line! In every way she seemed as radiant as her sunny bedchamber, from which one heard nothing of the many people two storeys below, only birdsong from a back garden one could view through her open windows as if enjoying serene Eden in the midst of London City.

Just as serenely Miss Nightingale greeted me. "Please, make yourself comfortable." She indicated an armchair pulled up to the far side of the bed, pleasantly situated near the windows. With unconcealed interest she studied me as I rounded her footboard and sat down.

"I was expecting someone a great deal older," she remarked, "given this." She held up the paper upon which I had written, in floral Morse code, *S.O.S.* "How do you know about my roses and daisies? But first, please, what is your name?"

Amazing, the way she exuded courtesy yet spared no honesty and wasted no time. Her manner allowed me to answer her truly. "Any name I could tell you, Miss Nightingale, I would have to invent, and at the moment I have small energy for dissembling."

She nodded as if this were an ordinary enough answer. Far back from her forehead, as if to show off the impeccable sheen and symmetry of her hair, she wore an odd sort of white kerchief that tied beneath her chin and lavished a cascade of lace from the crown of her head to the collar of her velvet bed-jacket. This singular headgear nodded along with her.

"I can see you are much distraught," she said softly—I was to learn that she was famous for never raising her voice, not once throughout her life or her years in the Crimea. "It would seem that your trouble somehow concerns me?"

"It might," I said, and without further ado, as concisely as possible I detailed the circumstances of Mrs. Tupper's abduction, starting with *CARRIER PIGEON, DELIVER YOUR BIRD-BRAINED MESSAGE AT ONCE OR YOU WILL BE SORRY YOU EVER LEFT SCUTARI*—the thornily handwritten message itself had disappeared along with my unfortunate landlady, but I knew the words by heart. Much as I knew the words that, according to Florrie, the bearded intruders had shouted at Mrs. Tupper: "We know you was a spy for the Bird!"

"Indeed, 'the Bird' is what they called me, those who opposed me," responded Miss Nightingale, "and they represented me as a bird-woman in their political cartoons." She spoke absently, with her back to me, for during my account she had turned around to rummage—I ought to explain that the headboard of her bed was actually a large, undoubtedly custom-made cubby-hole desk neatly packed with papers of all sorts, and that upon a green-draped table at her bedside more stacks of papers surrounded an electric lamp—an electric lamp! This was indeed a house of surprises, but I supposed that, driven to reform as she was, she had undertaken the expense so that she could write through the night. I had noticed that her hands, which looked far older than her face, were bent into crescents from constant writing.

Finding what she wanted, she turned back to me and showed it: *an elderly woman has been abducted by brigands,* et cetera, my note from the day before.

"Yes," I acknowledged. "I wrote that."

"And I answered it quite truthfully, dear. I simply do not recall Mrs. Tupper."

Reaching into my satchel, I brought forth Mrs. Tupper's wedding photograph, which I had carried along with me because of a presentiment that it might prove useful.

Miss Nightingale looked at this, and her gentle mouth formed an O of recognition.

"You remember her now?"

"Yes, dear, I do. I had forgotten, because she was not one of my regular couriers; I entrusted her only once, in an emergency, but her message was never delivered, and I have never found out why, or what became of her."

"So you *were* a spy," I whispered, much impressed.

"The commissioned officers of the army," she replied sweetly, "fought me, a woman and a civilian, with rather more passion than they devoted to the Russian enemy. I fought back."

"But I thought you and your nurses were there to help!"

She smiled rather sadly. "So we were, but the doctors and officers saw my presence as interference, and as a threat to their party-going, picnicking, polo-playing, horse-racing, high old good times. Which indeed it was. I had insane notions that the officers should spend their days looking after the welfare of their men, and the doctors should attend to the sick."

"You mean—they didn't?"

"The doctors—surgeons—excelled at lopping off the limbs of the wounded, but they never entered the fever-wards, such was their fear of themselves contracting the disease. Without supervision, the orderlies did as nearly as possible nothing, sometimes not even preparing food. So there, all alone except for one another, the sufferers lay in their own filth, their blankets heaving with lice . . ." Miss Nightingale broke off abruptly, her gaze focussing on me as if she were returning from a tragic past to a rather alarming present. "Tell me, my nameless friend: what ever became of the message I tried to send to Lord Whimbrel?"

I echoed, "Lord Whimbrel?"

"Yes, Sidney Whimbrel, a true statesman and my greatest ally."

How very interesting. I had just looked at his silhouette.

Miss Nightingale continued, "No reform could have been undertaken without him; he had the ear of the queen. He has long since passed away, but his good name remains to be protected. . . . Do you know, where is that missing message?"

"If it was the one basted to Mrs. Tupper's crinoline, I have it in my possession."

For the first time forsaking her erect posture, Florence Nightingale sank back against her pillows, studying me. From the music room on the floor below drifted the pleasant notes of a piano; someone was playing Mozart.

"You are clever," said Miss Nightingale in a way that made the statement neither praise nor censure. "Very well. You have my message that somehow went astray. I quite want it back, in order to avoid scandal."

"Scandal?"

"The reforms to which I have devoted my life are at last agreed upon and under way, with previous animosities forgotten; it would be disastrous were anyone to bring up the past. What would induce you—"

"I care nothing for politics. I simply want to know who has abducted Mrs. Tupper!"

"But I have no idea who that might be. And I quite want to find out, perhaps almost as much as you do, for if she were to tell them about the message—"

"Mrs. Tupper," I interrupted, frustration causing my voice to rise in marked contrast with the ever-level tones of my hostess, "is so exceedingly deaf that it will be very difficult for her to understand what they want of her. She was already deaf when you entrusted her with your ill-fated roses and daisies."

"Oh, dear." Miss Nightingale's face showed, very briefly, emotion. "How foolish of me not to realise. But I gave her a card with the address—"

"She can read coarse-hand, with difficulty, but not script."

"Oh, merciful heavens. But I assumed—whatever was I thinking?"

Softening my asperity, I acknowledged, "I imagine you had a great many pressing matters on your mind. In any event, as Mrs. Tupper understood not a word you said to her, one can assume she did not know what the card was for, or even realise she was carrying a message. The blackguards are currently cutting apart the blue dress you gave her, searching for something on paper. Now tell me, please, who are they?"

Florence Nightingale said again, "I don't know."

"But you could venture a guess!"

"As young Lord Whimbrel is just entering the House of Lords, I would guess that his enemies are trying to obtain this artefact in order to embarrass his family name. But equally I could guess that it could be any of the friends or descendants of the officers mentioned in the communication. Indeed, it would be difficult to name any involved person who would *not* like to find it, including myself." So disarming was this admission that it convinced me of her innocence. "I truly do not know. But I shall find out." She said this in the matter-of-fact tones of a woman who does as she pleases with her life. "I have already taken steps in the matter."

"How so?"

"When I received your note yesterday, it worried me. Even though I could not place Mrs. Tupper in my memory, it worried me exceedingly. So bethinking me of a rather well-known private consulting detective, I sent for him this morning. He should be here any moment now."

It was as if invisible hands clutched me by the throat, trying to strangle me. I felt Miss Nightingale watching my reaction, puzzled yet shrewd.

"Who?" I managed to gasp.

"You might as well tell me your name, dear, for I shall find it out eventually. The gentleman will oblige me, I am sure. I shall employ Mr. Sherlock Holmes."

CHAPTER
THE
TENTH

MY *BROTHER!* MIGHT WALK IN *AT ANY MOMENT!* AND
if he should find me here —

The kindly reader will please remember that I
had been under a great deal of duress, without much
rest or sufficient food — but truly, there is no excuse.
I should have addressed the problem with logic, reasoning it out. I did not.

I blush to admit that, simply put, I panicked.
With a yelp I shot to my feet, possessing no rational
plan of action, only a blind fervour to flee the premises; without a word of explanation or farewell I
darted around Miss Nightingale's bed towards the
door —

But, quite nimbly, Miss Nightingale threw back
her covers and jumped out of the other side of the
bed, her plump bare feet below the lace hem of her

nightgown engaging the floor as if it were a sprinter's starting block; in a few swift strides she reached the door before I could do so, and set her back to it.

This remarkable event—an invalid blocking my way—surprised me so much that astonishment trumped my senseless flight and halted me in the middle of the room.

"Of what are you so frightened?" Florence Nightingale asked.

At the same time I blurted, "What are you doing in a bed if you can walk?"

"Heavens, the impertinence of the younger generation!" But her sweet, low voice did not vary in the slightest. "Return to your chair, dear, and I will endeavour to explain."

Feeling a bit abashed, I did so.

"When I came home after nearly two years of tremendous exertion in the Crimea," remarked my hostess, tucking herself back into her customary seat under her covers, "I fell into total collapse, and quite believed I would die." A sensible enough expectation, as she had been past thirty at the time. "But as the weeks turned to months, indeed, to years, I found myself not only alive, but immersed once more in desperately needed reform, and there was so much important work to be done . . ."

As a rebel myself, at once I understood. "You did not care to spare time for the social amenities." Women of her class were expected to go calling, change for dinner, entertain houseguests, attend the theatre, and so on, ad infinitum, spending the better part of their lives serving, rather like epergnes, as useless, decorative objects.

"Exactly." She looked at me in a new way; recognition flew between us. "Now I have told you my secret; you must tell me yours. Why do you conceal your name, and why are you so afraid of Mr. Sherlock Holmes?"

I sincerely wished I could tell her the truth: Sherlock Holmes was my brother whom I adored, there was no one whose companionship I would rather have shared; the famous detective was —discounting my absent mum, Sherlock and Mycroft were all I had by way of family—yet their masculine ignorance caused them to feel that they must take me in charge and imprison me in a finishing school or some such den of feminine tortures. Therefore I dared not, could not, *must* not let them find me.

This was what I wished I could tell the wise and gentle Florence Nightingale, but I knew it could not be so. I said only, "I am terrified that he might find out about me." True enough, although meanwhile, quite desperately my mind cast about for some plausible lie. But at this crisis of all times my imagination deserted me; I could not begin to think what to say—

Amazingly, Miss Nightingale supplied for me the story I needed. Very gently she said, "It seems to me that the degree of your concern for, ah, Mrs. Tupper, is perhaps a bit unusual if Mrs. Tupper is indeed merely your landlady?"

Oh, good heavens. She thought I was an illegitimate daughter, protecting my (presumably) aristocratic father from the stigma of dalliance with—

Mrs. Tupper. How absurd. Poor, deaf, penny-pinching Mrs. Tupper, my mother?

Yet not so absurd, for truly, my sweet old landlady *was* more of a mum to me than my own mother—

Mum, from whom I had not heard since the incident of the bizarre bouquets, months ago. For whom I dared not search lest I actually find her and learn her true feelings, or lack of any, for me . . . It was not even necessary for me to lie, for long-suppressed injury in that moment attacked my heart with pain so severe, it assaulted my eyes. To my astonishment I found myself crying. The tears running down my face served as my answer.

Obviously a practical-minded person, Miss Nightingale responded by reaching into a night-stand drawer where apparently she kept a supply of neatly pressed, lace-edged handkerchiefs, for she handed me one. "Dear," she offered when I had composed myself a bit, "Mr. Sherlock Holmes is reputed to be the soul of discretion."

But shaking my head, once more I rose to my feet, this time remembering to pick up the leather carrying-case I had brought with me. "You'll excuse me, I'm sure."

Very kindly she did so.

Still in a most unmindful frame of mind, I made straight for the stairs.

A grave mistake. I should have, instead, sought out the narrow back steps that the servants used, gone down through the hidden regions of the house, and exited by way of the kitchen and the garden. But my senses had quite forsaken me; like a fool I ran straight down the same way I had come up, through the music-room and the drawing-room to the wide, main stairway, which I began precipitously to descend—

"But Miss Nightingale is currently engaged. Moreover, she never sees more than one person at a time," someone below was saying.

"She must make an exception in this case," responded a thrilling, familiar voice.

Nearly toppling with shock and in my hurry to halt, I clutched the banister and clung to it, feeling a bit weak.

"Watson is my right hand in these matters."

Sherlock! And the good Dr. Watson, of course, both of them at the base of the stairway, with Jack-anapes trying to tell them that only Holmes would be admitted.

And there, halfway down the stairs and no more than twenty feet away from them, I stood in plain sight and in great disarray of feature, gawping like a dead fish.

Dr. Watson, thank my lucky stars—for had he looked at me and recognised me as Dr. Ragostin's "secretary," that life would have been all over for me—the good doctor did not see me. He stood staring off towards one of the salons as if Mesmerised, perhaps by the presence of Mr. Gladstone.

But Sherlock's gaze, hawklike, flew to me. "Enola!" he cried with the most intense excitement and fixity of expression.

Because I could not stop looking at him, yet could not stay, I stumbled backwards up the steps, retreating.

But my brother Sherlock did not move. "Enola," he called. "Stop. Wait. Trust me. Please."

But I truly heard his words only afterwards, like

an echo in my dishevelled mind as I tore myself away, fleeing like a deer. Back through drawing-room and music-room I sped, and now, belatedly and in blind panic, I thought of the service stairway — but I could not find it! Past the grand piano, past the pedestal table, through passageways beyond, turning after turning I opened door after door to discover only antechambers, and I could hear Sherlock's energetic footfalls behind me, and his voice: "Enola! Confound the girl, where's she got to?" Evidently he had pushed past Jackanapes to run upstairs after me, and no doubt Watson had done the same, two against one — at the thought I sprinted even faster. I began to hear doors slamming as they followed my course. "Enola!"

At this point, as lackwit luck would have it, I blundered upon a winding little stairway — but it led only upward. So up I went, to find myself once again outside Florence Nightingale's door.

I opened it, shot into the room, and shut the door behind me.

From beneath her silken eiderdown comforter Miss Nightingale asked softly and sweetly, "Good-ness. Whatever is going on?"

Without answering, but seeing that the key stood in the keyhole, I locked the door. Then I darted across the room, around the end of Miss Nightingale's massive bed, to the windows that provided such a lovely treetop-level view of her back garden, at the same time unfastening my belt and slipping it through the handle of my satchel. Blessedly, the force of my fear had pushed me beyond fumbling and shaking to a state of extraordinary dexterity and energy. Speedily I refastened my belt, thereby strapping my precious baggage to my waist, even as I scanned my prospects for escape. After a hasty look, I chose one window and flung it open wide.

"Enola!" shouted my brother's voice right outside the door, and I heard him rattle the knob.

Miss Nightingale might, of course, have answered him, or got up out of bed, walked to the door, turned the key, and let him in. But she did none of those things. Instead, she lay where she was, watching, I suppose, as I clambered up upon the windowsill, leaned out, and launched myself like a monkey at the nearest tree branch.

My fingers found wood; my hands grasped. Three storeys above the ground I dangled, and descent would have perhaps seemed difficult had not worse difficulties goaded me so that I spent no time in contemplation. Like a veritable orangutan I swung, dropped, clutched another bough, dropped again, scrambled down, and so thumped to the ground. There I sped past a vegetable-garden, under a grape-arbour, behind a privy, and through a copse of linden trees to reach Miss Nightingale's wrought-iron fence. As I vaulted it, I caught a glimpse of Miss Nightingale—her oddly angled white headgear was unmistakable—at the window from which I had exited. Though I could scarcely see her expression from the distance, she appeared to observe me with serene interest. I saw no sign of Dr. Watson or my brother.

Once I had got well away—on the Underground, riding through a tunnel like a passageway to Hell, densely dark and choked with smoke—I finally had time and presence of mind to think.

Shades of perdition, Enola, now what?

At this very moment, I miserably surmised, my dear Sherlock was talking with my dear Miss Nightingale and putting too many twos and twos together. He would tell Miss Nightingale that I was his missing sister. Miss Nightingale would tell him that the missing Mrs. Tupper was my landlady. Heavens. With a helpless, sinking feeling that traversed the whole of my interior, I realised that I could not go back to Mrs. Tupper's house, for surely Sherlock, as part of his investigation, would find out where she lived.

Therefore, I now had no home.

Nowhere to go, really, for if I were followed—I could not really say, after all, where Sherlock was, or more villainously, he of the Classic Profile—certainly I must not chance leading either of them to Dr. Ragostin's office.

So I had no refuge.

And no plan.

Seldom had I felt so wretched—

Now come, Enola, this will not do.

The voice within my head was Mum's, yet mine. Even if I never saw my mother again, she lived on within me.

You are in danger of losing your freedom, but Mrs. Tupper is in danger of losing her life. After you have found your unfortunate landlady, then you may worry about yourself.

Taking a deep breath of the Underground's acrid air, I shut my eyes to the external darkness.

Now think.

Very well.

Who had kidnapped Mrs. Tupper?

Any of "the people involved," Florence Nightingale had said, might wish to secure the message so as to prevent scandal.

What "people involved"?

And what turn of events had involved them? Mrs. Tupper had lived for more than thirty years in peace with her crinoline crammed into her wardrobe; why now, suddenly, all this turmoil and trouble?

I had no idea.

However, thanks to the leather case which I had long since freed from my belt, I did still have the message.

I ought to finish decoding it.

CHAPTER
THE
ELEVENTH

I NEEDED A COPY OF THE MORSE CODE.

Where could I go to find one? The British Museum? Pfui. Den of nasty old men. I needed a haven, a sanctuary. I also, badly—as I had partaken of none of Miss Nightingale's scones—needed something to eat.

Finally my mind resumed functioning properly, for such a welcome thought occurred to me that I actually smiled. Exiting the Underground at the appropriate station, I sought a secluded corner and tidied myself a bit, then walked out again into London's streets, looking smartly about me. There was no sign of the pleasant-faced villain who had been following me, or of any other danger.

Making towards a main thoroughfare, I hailed a cab.

"High Street," I told the cabbie, for I did not wish to sing out for all the world to hear my precise destination.

A bit later, with a sigh of relief, I walked into London's, and perhaps the world's, first Professional Women's Club. I had not been here before, but I knew of the place by reputation. Just as men's clubs admitted no women, this small fortress admitted no men. But whereas men's clubs require new members to be sponsored by the old, the Professional Women's Club democratically welcomed any female who could pay the membership fee—which was quite substantial enough to keep out the undesirable classes.

After writing a cheque and receiving my membership card, I went on in, had a look around at the comfortable appointments of this sanctuary, nodded at a few other members (the younger ones, I noticed, clad much as I was), ordered tea and sandwiches, and settled myself in the library with volume *M* of the encyclopaedia.

Several hours, more tea, and another tray of sandwiches later,

```
. . . . / . * / . . . * / . V . * * . /. * . / *
* * / * * * / . . * . V . * * / . * . / . / . .
* . / * * * /. * . / * . . V . . . / . / . * .
. / . * . . / . . / * . / * * . V . . . / . . *
```

/ . * * . / . * * . / . * . . / . . / . / . . .
V * . * . / * * * / * . / . . . / * / . * / * .
/ * / . . / * . / * * * / . * * . / . * . . / .
V * * / . * / . * . / * . * / . / * V . * / .
* * . / . * * . / . / . * / . * . . / . / * . .
V * . * . / . * . / . . * / . . / * . * / . . . /
. . . . / . * / * . / * . * / . . . V . . . . /
. * / . * . . / . * . . V . * . / . * / * * . /
. * . . / . * / * . V * . / * * * V . * / . .
. * / . * / . . / . * . . V * * * / . . * . / .
. * . / . . / * . * . / . / . * . / . . . V * . *
. / . * / . * . . / * . . / * * * / . . * / . .
. V * * * / . * . V . * * / * * * / . * . / .
. . / . V . * * . / . * . / * * * / . . * . / .
. / * / * / . . / * . / * * . V . * * / . . . .
/ . . / . * . . / . V * * / . / * . V . . * .
/ . * . / . / . / * * . * . . . V . . . / * / . * /
. * . / . . . * / . V * . . / . . / . V * . . .
/ . / * * . V * . * * / * * * / . . * V . . *
/ . . . / . V . . / * . / . . * . / . * . . / . . *
/ . / * . / * . * . / . V . . . * / . * . V *
. . / . / . . . / . * * . / . * / . . / . * . /
. / * . / * * . V . . * . / * . V

turned out as follows:

HAVE PROOF WREFORD SELLING
SUPPLIES CONSTANTINOPLE

MARKET APPEALED CRUIKSHANKS
HALL RAGLAN NO AVAIL OFFICERS
CALLOUS OR WORSE PROFITTING
WHILE MEN FREEZE STARVE DIE
BEG YOU USE INFLUENCE VR
DESPAIRING FN

F.N. was of course Florence Nightingale, and *V.R.* was Victoria Regina, that is to say, Queen Victoria, but Wreford? Cruikshanks? Hall? Raglan?

"Crimean Conflict," in volume *C* of the *Britannica,* gave me to know that Cruikshanks was a general in that war, Hall the chief medical examiner, Wreford the army's remarkably inefficient purveyor, and Raglan the charming but utterly incompetent commander of the whole bloody mess, as exemplified by the Charge of the Light Brigade, hundreds of cavalrymen sent galloping into death due to an error in orders.

Looking up my suspects individually, I discovered that, like Lord Sidney Whimbrel, they were deceased, beyond my reach to locate or question.

What, therefore, was I now to do?

I had no idea, for presence of mind was difficult to maintain. Willy-nilly, even though I knew it was most unlikely that he could have traced me here, nevertheless I kept imagining Sherlock Holmes waiting to pounce upon me the moment I set foot outside the door. So disturbing were these thoughts that I could not sit still; I roamed the Professional Women's Club, the pleasant modern Oriental furnishings of reading-room, card-room, tea-room, and morning-room lost upon me as I fretted, imagining the most grotesque scenarios involving my brother Sherlock, Miss Nightingale, Mycroft, Dr. Watson, Scotland Yard, magistrates in white wigs, and ghoulish boarding school matrons, ad infinitum.

Enola, this will not do. I needed to think about Mrs. Tupper.

In order to force myself to do so, I realised, I must make a list.

So, taking the nearest seat—on a chintz-upholstered camel-back sofa, very chic, for I found myself in a charming little drawing-room where a few older women had gathered to chat—with paper and pencil in hand I began to write:

Where is Mrs. Tupper?
Who is Classic Profile?
Whose brougham took her away?
For what purpose? To speak with whom?

Et cetera. I started out, as I am sure the gentle reader can see, rather stupid, partly because I was so perturbed of mind and partly because of the distraction of pleasant, intelligent voices conversing all around me. For instance, a tall woman in a loose, comfortable "aesthetic" dress, with her grey hair flowing down her back, was saying, ". . . poor dear Rodney, such a pleasant, well-meaning gentleman, yet so sorely lacking in backbone, while his younger brother—"

"One must wonder," put in a different woman with a laugh, "how the theory of evolution would account for all the power's being given to the older brother, yet all the potency to the younger."

"That's not evolution, dear. That's our ridiculous laws of primogeniture."

"It's a shame," said another of the elderly women, "for Rodney will do almost anything Geoffrey says, and Geoffrey's strength of character is not always the *best* of character, or so I have heard."

Why was I listening to gossip of people I didn't even know, when I so badly needed to think? Yet I could not seem to shut my ears. I knew I should move to another room, yet did not.

A comfortable, matronly voice was saying, "Yes, his dear mother would be sorely dismayed. But then, good character in that family has generally run on the female side."

"Well, doesn't it generally in any civilised family?"

There was a ripple of laughter, during which the grey-haired aesthetic woman remarked, "Speaking of good families and characters, has anyone heard anything of Lady Eudoria Holmes?"

My mother! Hearing her name spoken aloud in such a comfortable, offhand fashion, I felt such a pang to my heart that for a moment I couldn't breathe, the world spun, I might faint—nonsense, I never faint; I must not miss a word. Making a great effort to control my speeding pulse and panting breath, I stiffened, eavesdropping intently, although I did not dare to look around at the speakers.

". . . no news of her at all since she disappeared. One does not know whether she is yet alive."

"Oh, I'm sure she's alive all right," put in a third, good-humoured voice. "She's far too strong minded to lie down and die just yet. I imagine she took off, as the youngsters would say."

A murmur of agreement sounded all around.

"I hope so," said the aesthetic woman. "I hope she's finally had a chance to live her life on her own terms."

These women had been friends of my mother. Friends of my *mother*! How peculiarly that simple thought, and their proximity, worked upon my sensibilities. Every fibre of my being ached with longing; how I wished I could feel as confidently as they that Mum was alive, and well, and enjoying herself.

"Perhaps she's gone overseas," said the good-humoured woman. "She always yearned to travel."

I had never known that!

"If so, let us hope she wanders far from the Balkans."

"Trouble there, as always?"

"There and here. I've heard that someone is endeavouring to stir up some sort of Crimean War scandal."

"Again? But why would anyone wish to dredge up that ruck of muck now?"

"Why, indeed."

"I'm sure I have no idea."

"Is it about Wreford again, perhaps? Any rehashing of that sordid affair would be most injurious . . ."

". . . today's progressive spirit . . ."

As they spoke of politics and reform, at last I was able to turn a deaf ear to their conversation, dismiss my thoughts and feelings regarding Mum (I had become quite adept at doing this), and write:

What turn of events started this dreadful business?

Who wanted Mrs. Tupper to deliver her message, and why?

Who stood to benefit? Enemies of reform?

To embarrass Florence Nightingale?

Who knew that <u>Mrs. Tupper, of all people,</u> had a message for "the Bird"?

That brought me up short, pencil poised in air as I stared at nothing, for at last, you see, I had asked myself the right question: Who knew of the existence of the cryptic crinoline? Given that no regular "carriers" for "the Bird" were involved, and Mrs. Tupper herself evidently did not realise her fine apparel's significance . . .

Who *knew*? Certainly not Wreford, Cruikshanks, Hall, or Raglan! Or their heirs.

When a message is sent in secret code, who must have knowledge of it? The sender. And the carrier — usually. And the person to whom the message is being sent might perhaps know that he should be in readiness to receive it.

Florence Nightingale knew.

I wrote:

*Miss Nightingale did not remember
Mrs. Tupper by name.
Miss Nightingale hired Sherlock
Holmes to find Mrs. Tupper.
Personal impression: Miss Nightin-
gale was not lying to me.
Reasonable supposition: Miss
Nightingale is not guilty.*

Very well. If Miss Nightingale had not kidnapped
my landlady—and, obviously, Mrs. Tupper had not
instigated her own abduction—there remained only
Lord Sidney Whimbrel.

"But he is Miss Nightingale's ally—or was, because he is now *deceased*!" I objected to myself aloud,
albeit in a whisper. And then, trying to joke, "Unless
his ghost—"

No joke. I had seen, and indeed I had been followed by, a man sufficiently identical to the late Sidney Whimbrel—or at least to his silhouette—to be
his ghost. But, as ghosts did not exist in the rational
world of a scientific perditorian, then that man—the
one who had burgled a blue dress in the night, and
who, according to Florrie, had carried off Mrs.

Tupper—might be Lord Sidney Whimbrel's kin, most likely his—

Son?

Nonsense, I argued with myself. The Whimbrels were amongst the most honoured and respected of titled British families. The idea of any scion of the Whimbrel family consorting with a common villain to abuse and kidnap my deaf and elderly landlady was preposterous.

But who else could it have been?

And hadn't Florence Nightingale said something about protecting the Whimbrel family name? And about young Whimbrel having recently been admitted to the House of Lords?

Also, hadn't the ill-matched pair of miscreants burgling Mrs. Tupper's house said something sarcastic about "His Lordship"?

"Oh, my stars and garters!" I whispered, realising that however preposterous it was, yet—yet it had to be. "*That's* what started this imbroglio!"

A few minutes later, in the Professional Women's Club library, I found myself quite thoughtful as I replaced *Boyles* upon the shelf and pocketed the address I had copied out of that useful reference book upon the members of the peerage.

My thoughts were manifold, astonished, and terrified. Such being the case, I also found myself contemplating with dark amusement the eighteenth-century philosophers, Alexander Pope and his ilk, who insisted that "everything is for the best in this best of all possible worlds"—in other words, if the baby dies, one must tell oneself that things would have been much worse had it lived; if thousands of orphans are starving in poorhouses, surely it is for some higher purpose, and—in my case—if I found myself hunted, on the run, unable to go home and sleep in my own bed, well, then, wasn't it wonderful that I had somewhere else to go tonight?

I had learned, amongst other most interesting revelations, the address of the Whimbrels' town house, where I quite hoped to find Mrs. Tupper.

CHAPTER THE TWELFTH

WHIMBREL HALL STOOD, A LORDLY, WHITE, four-towered mansion, in Mayfair only a block away from Florence Nightingale's house. At nightfall, still carrying my old brown leather satchel and still dressed in the same dark frock I had thrown on that morning, standing across the tree-lined street in the shadow of a friendly oak to study Whimbrel Hall, I wondered whether its address might have been the one, written upon a card, that Florence Nightingale had given to Mrs. Tupper amidst the horrors of Scutari so long ago.

The Italianate mansion, with its multiple quoins and brackets, looked temptingly simple to climb. But climbing, I had to remind myself, is not the answer to everything; even if I could scale the fence, evade the inevitable watchdog, swarm up the mansion, find entry, avoid detection or capture, and succeed in locating Mrs. Tupper, what then? I could hardly expect her to clamber out of a tower window and down its wall along with me.

Hmm.

Generally I managed to accomplish whatever I wanted either by stealth or by bribery. But in this case — as these people had quite enough money without any help from me — neither would do, and I needed to steel myself to try something I had never done before.

I had discovered, you see, from *Boyles*, that Lord Sidney Whimbrel had been survived by two sons, the elder of whom, and the new Lord Whimbrel, was named Rodney, and the younger of whom was named Geoffrey.

Now, *now*, the conversation I had chanced to overhear in the Professional Women's Club assumed utmost importance in my mind. Rodney? Geoffrey? Surely not coincidence, especially as the former had recently taken a seat in the House of Lords, providing reason to be gossiped about.

As Rodney, according to the ladies, was the good-hearted brother, I had decided my best course would be to appeal directly to him for Mrs. Tupper's release. If the younger, less scrupulous Geoffrey had not despatched her already! While I hated to think that any son of the revered Lord Sidney Whimbrel could be capable of such infamy, still, once he had kidnapped her and attempted to extract information from her, then—

Confound logic, anyway. It made my heart ache. And what if it had led me utterly astray? What if I were to sashay up to the door of Whimbrel Hall and either make an utter fool of myself, or—or never come out again?

Enola, you must be quite sure of yourself, or you will never pull it off. Now go over it all again. One step at a time.

And as I did so, in my mind, I noticed that I was not the only loiterer on the street. Puttering along, investigating the gutter as if he hoped to find something of value there, came a genteel greybearded sort of poor soul, not quite a beggar, his threadbare clothing that of a gentleman, cadaverous yet walking with a cane, tall but greatly bent by age, his untrimmed whiskers hiding most of his face while a truncated top-hat shadowed the rest. One should explain that when a top-hat becomes soiled by the wearer's perspiration and relegated to the second-hand clothing shops, the crown is removed, the stained part cut away, and the shortened crown reset on the brim. The greybeard's hat was a testament to this process, having undergone it at least three times.

Once before, on a freezing winter night, beside a

fire made in a washtub to warm the homeless, I had seen such a hat. Indeed, I had seen the same grey-beard, in only slightly different clothes. I recognised this interesting person, and as he approached, my heart began to pound in a most irrational manner, and I stood quite still in the shadow of the oak, terrified lest he see me.

Luckily, he hitched past me on the opposite side of the street without turning his head my way. Once I felt reasonably sure that he had not observed me, I breathed out.

Heavens. What next?

Never removing my gaze from him, I watched as he turned the corner, picking his way along the wrought-iron fence that surrounded Whimbrel Hall.

Even after he had passed out of sight, I did not move from the shadow of the oak. I waited to see whether I might work him into my plan, meanwhile reviewing my case as I had reasoned it out:

Lord Rodney Whimbrel takes his seat in the House of Lords.

He worries (or perhaps is induced by Geoffrey to worry) that a long-ago message his father never received may surface to embarrass him.

Geoffrey quite plans to handle Rodney's career however he pleases, perhaps to enrich himself, perhaps simply for the pleasure of wielding power.

Therefore Geoffrey, evidently a man with low compan-ions and a taste for illicit action, undertakes (along with a thuggish friend) to retrieve the troublesome missing message.

Failing to find the message, Geoffrey and friend kidnap Mrs. Tupper.

Lord Rodney Whimbrel, a "pleasant, well-meaning gentleman," is probably quite upset by this turn of events, but "lacking in backbone" has not done anything about it.

Perhaps I, Enola Holmes, by confronting him, might be able to —

Almost as if on cue, the genteel if impoverished greybeard reappeared at the far corner of Whimbrel Hall's wrought-iron fence.

Yes. It was as I thought.

Still I waited.

The elderly loiterer, having completed a circuit of the Whimbrel grounds, nevertheless limped back along the front of the property, covering the same ground again. Apparently, as I had suspected, he in-tended to stay in the neighbourhood for a while.

I had good reason to feel afraid. Very afraid, in-deed, of what I was about to do. Yet, as he ap-proached, a rueful warmth swelled my heart and made me smile.

Then, straightening myself like a soldier and holding my head high, I stepped forward. Across the street directly in front of the greybeard I strode, swinging my satchel and making sure that he saw me, although I did not look at him. Progressing up the pavement to Whimbrel Hall, boldly I mounted its marble steps, crossed the flambeaux-lit apron, and knocked at the massive mahogany front door.

The butler, opening this portal, regarded my solitary and spinsterish merino-clad personage with rather less favour than he might bestow upon an encroaching insect. He did not speak.

In very decided tones I declared, "I am here to see Lord Whimbrel," adding before I could be refused, "and I feel quite certain that he will wish to receive me."

The butler's eyebrows arched dangerously high, but my erect posture and crisp aristocratic accent somewhat reversed his first impression of me. As an aside, let me state that, while a talented mimic such as my brother Sherlock—or, dare I say it, myself—can ape a lower-class accent with ease, the opposite—a lower-class person speaking with an upper-class accent—is quite impossible, or at least to my knowledge has never been done.

Because of the quality of my aitches, then, the butler condescended to speak. "Your card, miss?"

"I carry no card and I bear no name." This pre-rehearsed line I flung out with quite an air of drama. "If you will allow me to compose and send a brief note to Lord Whimbrel, he shall see me."

The drama was part of my plan: I maintain that butlers, although they show none, do possess humanity, including curiosity. The man simply had to wonder what I was all about, and therefore stepped aside, waving me into Whimbrel Hall.

So large was the marble-floored entryway into which I stepped, and so cold, and so wallpapered, as it were, with elk skulls, samurai swords, Egyptian sarcophagi, elephant-foot umbrella-stands, odalisques, and bas-relief cupids and curios of every kind, that it might as well have been a museum. There were no chairs, nor did the butler offer me a seat in the library, but left me standing along with the statuary as he went off to fetch writing materials.

I took the opportunity to examine the outgoing post that had collected on a silver tray near the front door—and, yes! Amongst the letters I saw some addressed in black-inked, vicious, club-and-javelin-styled handwriting I could hardly mistake.

The sender: *The Honourable G. Whimbrel.* Geoffrey.

Repressing a shiver, I hoped I would not need to meet him.

Other letters, from *Lord R. Whimbrel,* displayed a rather pedestrian hand. Rodney appeared to be— well, one could not say for sure, especially as, being a Lord and Peer, he might have a secretary to address his post for him.

Hearing the butler returning, I transferred my gaze to a whatnot displaying cups made of ostrich eggs.

Approaching without a word, the servant presented to me a writing-stand furnished with good-quality paper, pen, inkwell, and its own candle, already lit, to provide light by which to write. But I scowled at these arrangements. "Bring me sealing-wax," I told him imperiously and also with an air, I hoped, of mystery.

"Of what colour, my lady?" I heard resentment and retort in his tone — resentment because he knew I was asserting myself over him, for plain candle-wax would have sufficed to seal the missive. Resentment also because its being sealed would prevent him from reading it as he bore it to his master. And retort because colour was symbolic; he was challenging me to show my intentions.

But at the same time, I noticed that I had been promoted from "miss" to "my lady."

"Why, red, of course," I told him. "Scarlet, rather than crimson." And let him make of that whatever he would.

As he went off to get the wax, I took pen in hand, concentrated on making my script large and strong, and wrote:

I have the message for the Bird.
Will exchange for Mrs. I.
without further ado. If turned
away, I will go to the police.

Leaving this unsigned, I blotted it dry and folded it so as to conceal its content before the butler, returning, had a chance to peek over my shoulder. Accepting from him the stick of red sealing-wax and lighting it at the candle, I dripped a blood-coloured puddle onto the paper's fold, where it congealed. Wishing I had a signet ring or something similarly dramatic with which to press it flat, I made do with the heel of my hand. When I was sure the seal had quite hardened, I gave the missive to the butler.

Off he went to deliver it to his master, leaving me standing beneath the carved wooden stare of several African war-masks.

For quite some time. I began to worry whether I had perhaps miscalculated. Should I have formulated my message in roses and daisies; would that have made a stronger impression? But no, it would not have been understood at all, for if Lord Rodney knew anything of the code, he—or, rather, his errand-boy, Geoffrey—would have recognised it on the crinoline.

I quite wished I knew a bit more of Lord Rodney. Was the namby-pamby handwriting his? Perhaps, because he seemed quite dependent upon Geoffrey.

Oh, dear. What if he were consulting with that villain right now?

Alas and indeed, such proved to be the case, for when the butler eventually returned and silently beckoned me to follow him, he escorted me into the shadowy, smoke-filled billiards-room—a place no proper lady would ever willingly set foot—and there, across the expanse of the green felt-topped gaming table, I found myself facing both young Whimbrels at once.

CHAPTER THE THIRTEENTH

LOUNGING WITH CIGARS IN HAND THEY RECEIVED me, leaning upon their cue-sticks, their attitude so insulting that I began to fear Lord Rodney might prove to be just such a villain as his younger brother. So similar were their oval, symmetrical faces and democratically blunt, pleasant features that one might have taken them for twins. I found no difficulty, however, in telling which was which simply by the expression of their eyes; Lord Rodney's gaze was open and anxious, whereas his brother Geoffrey's was hooded like a cobra.

I did not speak for a long moment. To tell the truth, I *could* not speak; in the terror of the encounter, all the words I had prepared turned coward and fled my mind like conscripts deserting a battlefield.

But I managed (I thought and hoped) to keep my spine stiff and my head high, and facing them I tried to glare rather than stare; I hoped my silence therefore seemed like scorn.

I hoped, also, that I seemed considerably older than my fourteen years. Such usually seems to be the effect of my height, my figure-augmenting underpinnings, and my sharp features.

Lord Rodney, I noticed, put down both his cue-stick and his cigar at once. And nervously he broke into speech. "So, you are the nameless one who sent in such a mysterious note, of which we understand nothing? I assure you, you are acting under some absurd misapprehension, my lady."

"Lady? That's no lady," Geoffrey corrected his brother with quite a preening air of indifference. "That's the lodger."

"Aha!" I cried. Bless Geoffrey's callous comportment and deplorable manners; he infuriated me, and instantly I found my voice. "And you say you know nothing of this affair? How dare you trifle with me." Although Geoffrey was the one who had aroused my ire, nevertheless I spoke straight to Lord Rodney, as if his younger brother were of no account — so better to irk *him*. "Kidnapping is a serious matter. Police and press can be hushed up with money, of course, but not Florence Nightingale. How do you think she would react if she knew what you have done? To whom do you think she would address her first hundred letters? And she *will* know if you do not act promptly to set the situation to rights. She has hired the famous detective, Mr. Sherlock Holmes —"

"Bosh and wind," broke in Geoffrey. "How can this girl possibly know anything of —"

I turned on him. "Florence Nightingale received me in her chamber, as you would know if you had followed me there the *second* time I visited her. And if you were not so busy abducting a defenseless, respectable, elderly woman —"

"I am not responsible for that!" Lord Rodney cried out in a tone that would have been more appropriate emanating from Mrs. Tupper. "I never expected —"

"Shut up!" Geoffrey barked at him.

But at the same time I looked upon Lord Rodney with a far more kindly gaze, reassuring him, "I quite believe you never expected the matter to go so far, or I would not be here talking to —"

"Balderdash!" the hot-blooded Geoffrey exploded. "He told me to get the message any way I had to. So I did what needed to be done. And now he will not let me dispose of the old woman. He thinks we can just let her go, and you, too, I suppose. Well, at least *one* son of our father has some guts."

130

With which coarse utterance, in a single moment, not giving even so much warning as a coiling snake might have done, he darted to seize me.

Were it not that the billiards table stood between us, he would have had me. But he needed to go around that obstacle, giving me just enough time to whip out my dagger and menace him with its stiletto-like eight-inch steel blade.

He stopped.

"You are not to lay hands on me," I told him softly between my teeth as he froze, staring, "for two reasons. This is one." I cocked my uplifted dagger so that the gas-light shone more prettily upon its blade. "The other is that my brother has seen me enter this house, and is waiting near the gate to see me come out again." By my fickle luck, arguably either good or bad, this was true; Sherlock Holmes had come here, presumably by following the same reasoning as I had, although arriving at his conclusions a bit more quickly: the greybeard loitering in the street was the great detective in disguise.

And, I realised rather to my own amazement, I *did* trust my older brother, with my life, although not with my freedom. "If I fail to appear within a reasonable time, he will take action, and I assure you, you will find him a most formidable adversary."

Silence followed, and there we stood like a tableau, I with my back to the wall and my dagger raised, Geoffrey poised a mere two paces from me with sheerest evil in his eyes, and Lord Rodney on the other side of the billiards table—I did not of course chance a look at him, but I imagined he might be wringing his hands.

Everything depended on Lord Rodney.

And with that thought, the essence of my planned appeal came back to me, and I addressed him with it, although necessarily in a very abbreviated form. "Lord Rodney," I said levelly, "yours is the title of Lord Whimbrel; yours is the seat in the House of Lords; yours is the authority." With my left hand I reached into the pocket centred under the front drapery of my dress, where I had at the ready what I needed. I drew it out and— feeling at the wire hanger on its back to make sure I had it upright, for I could not look away from the dastardly Geoffrey, not even for an instant—I held it up, facing it towards Lord Rodney: confronting him with a small portrait in silhouette.

The Honourable Sidney Whimbrel, at Embley, Summer 1853.

His father.

"Lord Rodney Whimbrel," I addressed that peripheral individual, "I show you the likeness of a great statesman. His place deserves to be held by a worthy scion. How much longer—"

Geoffrey shouted at him, "You fool, don't just stand there! Hit her with your stick!"

"How much longer are you going to allow your brother's regrettable impulses to shame your father's name?"

He did not answer either of us, but out of the corner of my eye I saw him move, reaching for something. Stiffening, I put the silhouette down upon the billiards table lest I need both hands to defend myself—but no, he was not hefting a cue-stick. Rather, he had grasped the bell-pull, summoning a servant—probably the butler.

Another tall, strong, and most unprepossessing man.

Oh, dear.

The billiards-room door opened, and indeed so, I glimpsed a black-suited, poker-straight looming form, but I did not dare to look away from Geoffrey, not even for an eye-blink to see whether the butler had managed to remain expressionless.

And how long the moments seemed, how the silence stretched as I held my ground, waiting to see what Lord Rodney would do.

I am sure the butler quite wondered the same thing, although his voice sounded no less wooden than usual as he inquired, "You rang, my Lord?"

He addressed Lord Rodney, of course, but Geoffrey burst out, "For God's sake, Billings, fetch the footmen and a rope so we can quell this ugly wench—"

"Silence. I give the orders." Lord Rodney's voice wavered; nevertheless, his were the words that mattered. "Billings, kindly escort the Honorable Geoffrey to his chambers and have him remain there."

"What!" Geoffrey roared, turning on his brother and making towards him as if to attack him much as he wished to attack me. But Billings strode in and caught him by both arms from behind. Geoffrey shouted and flailed as if he intended to create considerable unpleasantness; Lord Rodney rang the bell again as he retreated. "By all means have the footmen assist you if necessary," he told Billings, and gesturing for me to come with him, he exited the room by another door.

"Do please put that frightening thing away," he told me the moment we set foot in the corridor.

I sheathed my dagger, but he seemed unwilling to turn his back on me, having me walk ahead of him as we made our way—upstairs? I had expected he would take me to a parlour or library or some such quiet place where we could sit and negotiate terms, mutually agreeing how to exchange my message for his hostage. But instead, up three flights of stairs we went without a word—wide and gracious stairs in the front of the house, not narrow back ways, so I did not begin to feel afraid until he led, or rather herded, me towards what I realised must be the top of one of the mansion's white marble towers.

Quite a good place for a makeshift prison.

I stopped where I was, turning to look at Lord Rodney's face.

And he halted, submitting to my scrutiny. Although very pale, and rather down in the mouth, he seemed composed. "If you wish me truly to be a Lord Whimbrel worthy of my father's name," he said, sounding not particularly strong but not too unsteady, either, "then you must agree to trust me. Done?"

And indeed, what was my alternative? To run away, leaving Mrs. Tupper to her fate? I hesitated only a moment before I answered. "Very well. Done."

With a weary nod he beckoned me forward to a narrow, heavy dark door. He produced a large key and turned it in the lock. Opening the door and standing aside, he motioned for me to enter.

I confess that I did not immediately walk in. Rather, I paused in the doorway of a small room furnished with numerous gas-lamps and sconces of candles, by the shining light of which I saw, not necessarily in this order:

Colourful chintz curtains.

A brass bed plump with pillows and quilts.

A vase full of fragrant apple-blossoms.

A plate of fresh strawberries.

A young maid sitting in a straight chair with her hands folded, waiting, as if something else might be needed.

A table upon which stood a stereopticon.

Beside an overstuffed easy chair.

In which, propped up by pillows as she viewed the clever three-dimensional images that had been provided for her amusement, sat Mrs. Tupper.

My feelings can scarcely be imagined, so strong and strangely mixed were they—relief so great that it made me weak in the knees, but also astonishment, irrational outrage, and a bit of envy— nobody gave *me* fresh strawberries or a stereopticon! Altogether I found myself nearly overcome by disorderly emotion which I had no time to discipline, for at the moment I saw Mrs. Tupper, she also saw me. With a mynah-bird cry she tottered to her feet and toppled towards me. I hurried forward lest she fall. She hastened to fling her arms around my waist.

"Miss Meshle!" She was weeping, and so, I must admit, was I, and the maid rose, curtsied, then exited the room, no doubt at Lord Rodney's silent signal. He stood just inside the door, waiting for the tempest to calm, with the look of one who has forgot his umbrella.

"Oh, Miss Meshle," iterated Mrs. Tupper, "oh, Miss Meshle, I'm that glad to see you, I am, Miss Meshle!"

Patting her head, which came barely to my shoulder, I noticed that she wore a crisp, new white housecap with lavender ribbons, and a new lavender dress to match. Speaking wryly in an attempt to dry out my feelings, I said, "It appears you have not been mistreated."

"Eh?" She put her head up like a turtle, a hand behind one ear.

Instantly all seemed so annoyingly normal that I calmed. I sighed deeply, then bawled directly into her ear, "You're all right?"

"Oh! Yes, thanks to this'un." Still tearful, she bobbed towards Lord Rodney. "'E's as kind a gennelmun as ever wore spats. But t'other'un, 'e wants to throw me in the river!"

"I have never in my life worn spats. And t'other'un," said Lord Rodney with an undertone of dark humour in his voice, "will be on a ship to Australia within the week."

Mrs. Tupper, who of course could not hear him, cried, "I been that scared, I 'ave!"

"Poor dear." Of course she had been terribly frightened, not knowing who these people were, or what they wanted, or which one was older, or younger, or more likely to get his way. "There, there." Muttering soothing inanities even though I knew quite well she could not hear me, I patted her humped back, speaking over her head to Lord Rodney. "An excellent idea. Your brother's talents will be much more useful and appreciated in such a wild place," I told him quite sincerely.

But I am afraid I cannot remember what he replied, for when I directed my eyes towards him, I saw a face looking in at a window behind him.

This was most startling, considering that we stood in a room four storeys above the ground. Equally startling was the face, its sharp nose actually pressed to the glass, making a white triangle amidst a wrack of grey hair.

Yet, rather than jumping and screaming, I smiled. Indeed, I gave my brother Sherlock quite an impudent look, imagining how he must be hanging on to the stonework outside. I dearly wished to stick out my tongue at him, but I could not, of course, or Lord Rodney would have seen.

Instead, I inquired of that nervous person, "Might we go downstairs?"

"Of course, Miss Meshle—that is your name, is it not?"

It was not, strictly speaking, so I replied sweetly, "There would be no point in my denying it."

"Mrs. Tupper possesses in you a remarkably loyal lodger, Miss Meshle. By all means, let us go where we can all sit down. Shall I order some tea?"

"That would be delightful."

Chapter the Fourteenth

THE NEGOTIATIONS, IN A RATHER GRANDIOSE sitting-room, took some time. Lord Rodney required a great deal of reassuring, yet at the same time I wished him to give Mrs. Tupper a great deal of money; those two objectives were difficult to reconcile or to accomplish simultaneously.

I tried to reason with him. "Mrs. Tupper has no idea of your name, or your brother's name, or who you are, or where she has been taken—is this not so?"

He looked ruefully upon the old woman, who, much comforted by tea and my presence, had dozed off in her blue velvet armchair. "Yes, I believe that is correct."

"Doubtless you have noticed, also, that she is somewhat hampered in her ability to communicate."

"True."

"And she has not a vindictive bone in her body. Once safely home, with some recompense for her trouble, she will say nothing more of the matter. No East Ender ever willingly speaks to the police."

"What about you? In your note you said you would go to the authorities."

"I said what I felt was necessary at the time. Surely, now that you have met me, you understand that I can be discreet."

"To the contrary. I understand mostly that you can brandish a dagger."

"Just as any sensible woman would do under the circumstances."

He eyed me doubtfully. "You're no ordinary woman."

I fear I rolled my eyes. "I have trusted you. Now you must trust me. Once you have provided for Mrs. Tupper's financial security in her old age—"

"You want no money for yourself?" he interrupted suspiciously.

"None, I assure you."

"And you will tell Florence Nightingale nothing of any of this?"

"Nothing at all. I see no reason why I should ever set foot in her gracious home again."

"Then you promise me no ill consequences?"

"None at all." For myself, I was thinking bitterly, the consequences would be far worse than any he faced: because Sherlock knew of Mrs. Tupper, I would have to give up lodging with her and find myself a new place at once—unless, as might very well be the case, Sherlock were to catch me tonight, immediately upon my exit from Whimbrel Hall! All too aware that he was waiting for me, from time to time I caught a glimpse of him skulking outside the sitting-room windows.

Focussing with difficulty on Lord Rodney, I continued. "Certainly you can see that I bear you, personally, not the slightest ill-will. And for the house of Whimbrel, I cherish only the greatest respect. Indeed, I share Florence Nightingale's high opinion."

And so I wheedled for a considerable length of time. Eventually, after much coaxing and many promises, a rather handsome sum changed hands— I am sure that poor Lord Rodney believed, despite all my protestations to the contrary, that he was bribing me for silence—and I reached into my satchel and presented His Lordship with a tangle of blue ribbons embroidered with posies.

Understandably, he seemed taken aback. "What's this?"

"The missing message," I told him, "and here is the way I worked it out." I handed him the papers on which I had pencilled the code. Then I stood and walked over to touch Mrs. Tupper upon the shoulder, awakening her as I told Lord Rodney, "We should go now. I would be obliged if you would summon your carriage."

This was very necessary in order for me to escape my brother, for certainly Mrs. Tupper could not run or climb trees with me.

"I will do nothing of the sort." Lord Rodney sounded all too much as if he had thoroughly discovered he was indeed Lord Whimbrel; worse, he sounded peevishly wrought, as if he had expected something more to his masculine taste for his money. "You are going nowhere. Sit down and explain this nonsense."

"It's not nonsense." Although I should have known better, his temper caught me off guard, and my tone heightened to match his. "It has cost me a great deal of trouble, and—"

And Heaven only knows how things would have gone if it were not that, just then, a considerable crash resounded upstairs, and shouts, and the sound of feet pounding down the stairway, and a great deal of hubbub throughout the house as Geoffrey Whimbrel thundered into view, pursued by two footmen in buckle-shoes, stockings, knee-breeches, red jackets, and white powdered wigs. It would make an interesting study, why decorative servants must dress like the upper classes of the prior century. Most impractical. One footman's wig had been jolted askew and the other's flew right off as they pelted after his younger lordship. At the foot of the stairs the butler, Billings, joined the pursuit, bellowing unnecessarily, "He's broken out, my Lord!"

Already Lord Rodney had jumped up and darted towards the large, museum-like entryway through which his younger brother was running for the door. I also leapt up to go see, and Mrs. Tupper, at her best hunchbacked speed, did likewise. Indeed, shrieks and yells both feminine and masculine sounded from the direction of the kitchen and other nether regions as the entire household came running to observe the fracas. Seemingly out of nowhere a crowd assembled.

The two footmen, the butler, and Lord Rodney attached themselves to Geoffrey like bulldogs to a bear, but even their combined strength failed to halt his charge for the door. They clung to his coattails and clawed at his shoulders as he lifted the latches and turned the bolts, flinging the door open —

Clearly visible in the firelight of the flambeaux, on the marble apron just outside the door waited a remarkably tall, angular personage with a great deal of unkempt grey hair and beard.

I was perhaps the only one not totally astonished.

Except, apparently, Geoffrey. Enraged or desperate beyond such petty sentiments as surprise, he took no pause. Tearing free of the annoying people clinging to his back, he hurtled out the door as if to run right over the greybeard.

But he ran instead into what might as well have been a bolt of lightning. Most swiftly and unexpectedly the tall man slashed a chopping blow with his edgewise hand, one long leg extended—alas, I cannot fully describe the manoeuvres which I believe, from references in the writings of Dr. Watson, demonstrated the Eastern martial art of "jujitsu," nor can I detail the single-handed combat that landed Geoffrey on his back with the greybeard atop him, nor could I take pleasure in my brother's prowess or in the astonishment of the onlookers observing a thin old man knocking down a strong young aristocrat. I retain only the most fragmentary memory of any of this, for I did not stay to watch.

Instead, taking Mrs. Tupper by the hand, I hurried her towards the back of the house, intent on getting out there while everyone, including Sherlock—especially Sherlock—was busied at the front.

Although Mrs. Tupper kept up the best pace she could, it was not good enough, so I actually caught her up in my arms, slung her slight weight over one shoulder, and ran with her through hallways and serving-ways that were utterly deserted. So also was the kitchen. Out its door and up the steps of its area we scuttled, making a hasty escape through the usual maze of outbuildings—summer-kitchen, tool-shed, dog-kennel, carriage-house—until we reached the back gate, which stopped us but a moment; such safeguards, meant to keep intruders *out,* are simple enough to open from the inside. Still carrying Mrs. Tupper—although I confess I was starting to breathe quite hard—I trotted along a back lane until I achieved a street.

There, under the murky glow of a gas-lamp and out of sight of Whimbrel Hall, I felt a bit more secure. Setting Mrs. Tupper down on her own two tottery feet, I stooped to examine her for signs of damage. "Are you all right?" I asked—softly, for I did not wish to attract the attention of the neighbourhood by shouting—I hoped Mrs. Tupper might be able to read my lips.

She seemed to. "Miss Meshle," she quavered, her voice as well as her eyes rather watery, "I'm so ever-lastingly obliged to you, I—"

"Shhh." I had to look away from her, for in that moment it truly smote me, with great pain to my heart, that I must leave her.

And then I, Enola, whose name backwards spells "alone," would be even more lonely than ever, for

146

Mrs. Tupper—my deaf, elderly landlady who served the most dreadful suppers—had nevertheless been, sometimes, like a mother to me.

Oh, Mum. Where are you?

It was the worst thing I could have thought, for my mother . . . more and more, although I tried to deny it, I felt irrationally certain that I would never see Mum again, that she had succumbed to old age, and the Gypsies, illiterate nomads, had left her somewhere in an unmarked grave.

Stop it, Enola.

Barely holding back tears, I took Mrs. Tupper's arm and hurried her along the street until at last, seeing a cab approaching, I hailed it.

Inside the concealment of the four-wheeler I handed over to Mrs. Tupper the money I had extracted from Lord Rodney Whimbrel, shushing her astonished protests; I needed to feel sure that she would never go hungry or lack for means. I saw to it that she tucked the hundred-pound notes deeply into her bosom. When we arrived at her lowly hovel in the East End of London, we both got out, but I ordered the cab to wait.

Leaving Mrs. Tupper downstairs to exclaim over the ruin of her home, I ran up to my room—soon no longer to be mine anymore—where I thrust into a carpet-bag only my most compromising or irreplaceable possessions: my wig, facial emollients, and various other essentials of disguise, my extra dagger, all my money, and the little handmade booklet, decorated with watercolour flowers, which had been my mother's last gift to me.

Running downstairs again with baggage in hand, I found Mrs. Tupper—showing more intelligence than I had credited her—waiting by the door, clutching to her bosom the carved wooden box that contained her meagre lifetime of documents and mementos, with the most forlorn look on her face.

"Miss Meshle, don't leave me 'ere alone, not after wot's 'appened," she implored. "I don't feel safe 'ere an' it ain't 'ome to me no more. Take me wit' you."

Time seemed to spin in a circle, then come to a teetering, off-balance halt. Take her along? If only my mum had taken me along with her!

But where—in what way—how could I possibly—

Explosively my mind countered its own consternation: Never mind the difficulties. Blast and confound Sherlock Holmes and Mycroft Holmes, too, hang any danger they might pose to me, I simply could *not* leave Mrs. Tupper.

Time whirled into motion, centred now. "Come along then, quickly!" Her crumpled old face cleared as I took her by the hand. Together we scuttled to the cab.

"Where to now, miss?" the driver asked.

Quite cheerfully I told him, "I have no idea!" Although surely I would, soon enough; I had learned to trust the peculiar workings of my heart and mind. "Just drive west."

Thus, forth we sallied into London City.

May, 1889

"I CANNOT CREATE EMBROIDERY ANYMORE,"
Florence Nightingale remarks with nostalgia but no
self-pity as she fingers a quantity of blue ribbon,
winsomely stitched with five petalled daisies and
little round roses, that her visitor has deposited upon
the counterpane of her bed. "My hands can no longer manage a needle." Indeed, they are misshapen
from constant writing, which is far more important.
Needlecraft is a frivolous pursuit. Such are the
thoughts of the once-famous Lady with the Lamp
as she turns her placid attention to her visitor. "You
say Lord Rodney Whimbrel wishes me to have
these. Why?"

Standing over her—for he has not been invited
to have a seat; even though she has engaged Sher-

lock Holmes to help her, still, his intrusion must not last long—the famous detective responds, "Lord Whimbrel hopes in this way to convey that the matter is ended completely, and that he remains your most loyal admirer."

"And he wishes me to forget how the matter began?"

"Although Lord Rodney takes responsibility, Miss Nightingale, still, one must consider his brother Geoffrey the instigator. And he shall instigate no more. His other choices being only worse, he has agreed to take ship to the colonies."

"Then I shall withhold judgment, and hope that Lord Rodney shows increased moral fortitude in the future."

While speaking, thoughtfully Florence Nightingale scans the tall, lean, angular man of action, so exceedingly vertical in her serene horizontal surroundings. In his "Miss Nightingale" she has heard gallantry, yes, but also a hint of condescension. She had not intended to speak to him of a certain tall girl of action, but . . .

Thrusting the embroidered ribbons to one side, she gestures for Sherlock Holmes to take a seat. When he has done so, she tells him in her customary soft and gentle manner, "Doubtless you wonder why I did not attempt to stop your quite remarkable sister from taking such precipitous departure a few days ago. No"—as he scowls and flings up one gloved hand, trying to halt this conversation—"let me speak. While I had no idea, until you told me so, that—Enola, is that her name?—Enola is a mere child of fourteen—"

With far less than his usual courtesy, Sherlock Holmes interrupts. "It would not matter if she were, as she appears to be, twenty-four! Would you let *your* daughter, if you had one—"

But Florence Nightingale interrupts the interruption, sweetly and apparently tangentially: "I knew your mother, you realise, Mr. Holmes."

Evidently he does not realise, and the revelation staggers him somewhat, for he sits back in his arm-chair and watches the invalid—a remarkable woman, with her smooth face, her sleek hair parted in the old-fashioned manner and shown off by her peculiar headgear—he studies Florence Nightingale from beneath troubled brows.

"Eudoria Vernet Holmes. A thoroughly admirable woman," the Lady with the Lamp speaks on, "totally and efficiently committed to reform. She chose to espouse women's rights, whereas I turned my attention to the plight of the sick and wounded, but we quite respected each other. Have you had any word from her, Mr. Holmes?"

"You are aware that she is missing, then? No, I have heard nothing." He hesitates only an instant before asking, "Have you?"

Ah! He did care for his mum.

"I am sorry to say I have not. Perhaps she has run off to the Crimea?" Mocking herself slightly, Florence Nightingale speaks lightly yet with care. "Being who I am, I would hardly restrain any woman, no matter how tender her years—"

Sherlock Holmes leans forward, cutting her off with a gesture like a jujitsu chop. And, interestingly, he speaks not of Enola Holmes, but of Eudoria. "My brother and I had quarrelled with Mother. Now, looking back, it all seems like a great deal of non-sense," he says bluntly and with unexpected bitter-ness. "Still, there was no reason for her to—"

"But can you not see," Florence Nightingale in-terjects with greatest soft-spoken authority, "that from her point of view, there was every reason, obvi-ously? And your sister, also, a few days ago, seemed to have the most compelling reason for her actions." Miss Nightingale hesitates, then decides to say it. "She seemed quite terrified of you."

Although he does not actually wince, she sees how her words strike like a blow. Leaning his fore-arms upon his knees, he clasps his hands and looks down at them.

Patiently Miss Nightingale waits for some other response.

"I cannot deny it," he says at length, "yet I cannot by any application of my considerable mental abilities understand why she fears me so. I would never do anything to harm her, and she knows that, I'm sure; she has from time to time displayed unmistakable affection for me."

A good nurse knows when to be silent and let the patient talk. Florence Nightingale waits some more.

"My brother Mycroft and I want for the girl only what would be in her own best interests," Sherlock Holmes goes on. "Some further education, at a good boarding school—"

"Ah!" Suddenly and completely Florence Nightingale understands. "You have threatened her with boarding school!"

Sherlock Holmes raises a puzzled, almost boyish gaze to her face. "Why, what ever is the threat—"

"Good heavens, didn't your mother tell you?" Although, actually, his ignorance is no more extensive than that of other males. "The sufferings of an upperclass girl in a typical boarding school are only slightly less severe than those of an imprisoned criminal upon a treadmill. I speak of painful physical rigours that result invariably in deformity and sometimes in death."

The great detective sits with his mouth ajar, evidently at a loss.

"My good man," Florence Nightingale tells him gently, "please forgive me for being quite unconscionably blunt and, indeed, coarse, but I am an old woman, and as such, I will say what others won't: thumbscrews are merciful compared with a fully tightened corset."

It is a word never spoken in polite society, much less in mixed company. Hearing it, the man of action raises both hands in protest, and a flush of pink can be seen in his aquiline face. But Florence Nightingale perseveres.

"Why," she challenges his intellect, "do you think fashionable women constantly faint? And die of the slightest ailment, much less childbirth? Or occasionally fade away and succumb even before reaching childbearing age? It is because they are compressed at the waist in a practise no more civilised than the binding of a Chinese woman's feet! Far beyond comfort, beyond health . . . small wonder your sister fears you. In fleeing boarding school, she is literally running for her life."

"But—but it simply cannot be as bad as you say," exclaims Sherlock Holmes. "Tradition—elegance—generations of ladies have survived—"

"One might with similar logic say that traditionally, generations of soldiers have *survived* wars," remarks Florence Nightingale. But then, with the diplomatic instinct that has seen her through a lifetime of dealing with authoritative males, she turns the conversation mildly aside. "I have never had a child, but I *have* had a sister, and I quite sympathise with your concern for yours," she assures her visitor. "Perhaps Mrs. Tupper can tell you something of her whereabouts?"

From downstairs the piano resounds, filling the house with the majestic measures of Beethoven, and although neither the great detective nor the great reformer can see Mrs. Tupper right now, both know where she is: sitting directly beside the instrument, entranced and ecstatic because she can actually hear the music.

With a bleak chuckle Sherlock Holmes leans back in his chair. "No, there is nothing to be got out of Mrs. Tupper, as I'm sure Enola knows quite well. The sheer audacity of the girl," he goes in, in tones of mingled wonder and exasperation, "never ceases to astonish me. For her to venture here when a mere block away at Whimbrel Hall I was still casting about for her trail, for her to drop off the old woman as if she were an expected visitor—"

Smoothly Florence Nightingale puts in, "But I am delighted to care for Mrs. Tupper in her old age."

"Very good of you, I am sure," he retorts rather abrasively, but then he corrects his tone. "Would you also be so good as to send for me if my sister comes here to visit her?"

Florence Nightingale scarcely hesitates before she speaks, seemingly not addressing his question. "You have an older brother, I recall."

"Mycroft. Yes."

"Also a bachelor, a recluse, a misanthrope, indeed, a misogynist, and quite set in his ways?"

How on earth does she know so much? The great detective scowls. "I flatter myself that I have some small influence over him."

"Nevertheless, Mr. Holmes, his is the legal authority. Now, how would I know if your sister were to come here?" says Florence Nightingale with sweetest, wide-eyed innocence. "I never go downstairs."

Sherlock Holmes, who also possesses the instincts of a diplomat, knows when an impasse has been reached. Without further comment he rises. "Miss Nightingale, I am delighted to have met you," he tells her, standing by her bedside to take one of her half-crippled hands and bow over it. "If I can ever be of further service, please do not hesitate to call upon me."

His thoughts, however, as he takes his leave, are far from delighted. As he stalks past Mrs. Tupper in her rocking-chair by the piano, Sherlock Holmes considers that Enola is sure to visit that elderly woman. Therefore, by deploying the Baker Street Irregulars, his troop of street urchins, to watch the house, he has a very good chance of catching his sister, confound and bless the daredevil, oh-so-clever girl—

But then what?

Is there possibly any truth to the distressing and indelicate things that Florence Nightingale has told him?

If Mum were here, might she tell him likewise?

Ye gods! Is he losing his world-famous mind, wishing now that he could ask for the advice of his mother, which he would have utterly disregarded a year ago?

His mother, whom he has been unable to locate?

Confound everything! Why did that eccentric woman run away? And why did his sister then flee as well, and why does she continue to do so? Perhaps— and this is a very difficult thought for the man of action to admit—perhaps he has been going about things all wrong, thinking he must take Enola in hand?

For her own good?

As he exits Florence Nightingale's gracious home, for the first time the great detective's brilliant mind asks what, really, his sister's *own* good might be. Boarding school, education in the social graces, introduction to polite society, preparation for marriage — however proper and traditional, still, are these necessarily the best plans for *Enola*?

INTERNATIONAL MORSE CODE

A	•—	N	—•	1	•————	Ñ	——•——
B	—•••	O	———	2	••———	Ö	———•
C	—•—•	P	•——•	3	•••——	Ü	••——
D	—••	Q	——•—	4	••••—	,	——••——
E	•	R	•—•	5	•••••	.	•—•—•—
F	••—•	S	——•	6	—••••	?	••——••
G	——•	T	•••	7	——•••	;	—•—•—
H	••••	U	••—	8	———••	:	———•••
I	••	V	•••—	9	————•	/	—••—•
J	•———	W	•——	0	—————	-	—••••—
K	—•—	X	—••—	Á	•——•—	'	•————•
L	•—••	Y	—•——	Ä	•—•—	()	—•——•—
M	——	Z	——••	É	••—••	_	•——•—•

Author's Note

Concerning the Crimean War and Florence Nightingale, I have done my best to adhere to documented facts. However, there is no evidence that Florence Nightingale engaged in secret communications; her use of code is my own invention. After the war, the famous nurse did spend the rest of her life as an invalid. Why so is a question hotly debated among scholars. As no one is certain what caused Florence Nightingale's peculiar conduct, I took the liberty of giving it my own interpretation. She did indeed live in Mayfair, with a view of Hyde Park, although my description of her house is necessarily imaginary, as the original is gone. While it is true that Florence Nightingale was quite influential in politics and affairs of court, Lord Whimbrel and his sons are fictitious characters.